MANNY, MY LOVE

a rare love story, inspired by true life events

MANNY, MY LOVE

a rare love story, inspired by true life events

Norman Gate

First published in India in November 2021

Copyright © Norman Gate, 2021

ISBN: 978-0-6453148-0-9

Norman Gate asserts the moral right to
be identified as the author of this book.

This is a love story based on true life events. It's a story of two
lovers each with desires, fears and choices to reckon with. It's
a story that strongly supports the truism—love can happen to
anyone, anytime. Age and situation are no bar to love.

Published by: Self Published

Introduction

Love. It's magical. It's the most beautiful feeling in the world. It connects us all beyond anything else. No word in any language has ever been able to contain love, that's how powerful the emotion is.

In all likelihood, you would have experienced love at some point in your life. Blessed are those who live with love. There are also those who live in hope of finding love and those who've given up on love.

Manny, My Love, is a love story based on true life events. It's a story of two lovers each with desires, fears and choices to reckon with. It's a story that strongly supports the truism— love can happen to anyone, anytime. Age and situation are no bar to love.

When love happens, don't hold back. The only way to live is to surrender to love.

October 30, 2069

Rugged up in her favourite rocking chair on a rather chilly day, Manny gazed at the tangerine tree in her backyard. It had been a constant in her life ever since she had migrated to Australia 47 long years ago. Manny badly needed something to hold on to as she struggled to ride out the wave upon wave of memories possessing her.

Gulshan. Piggy. Her Piggy. Her world since she had left India. He had gone in a blink of an eye. Who would fill her world now?

Manny could feel Piggy; even smell him in the jumper she was wearing. Why not? It had only been a week since Gulshan had passed.

Yesterday, at his funeral, in front of her family and neighbours, she had held herself up. But it had been so hard when all she had wanted to do was cry. Today, she badly needed to let out her pain.

Manny had thought that the gentle movement of the chair might help soothe her distraught mind but no. Her hands had been resting on the chair, lightly grasping the arms. As her thoughts got the better of her, the grasp became a clutch. Her hands whitened. Her bosom heaved. She found it increasingly hard to breathe. Finally, Manny could no longer keep her emotions reigned in. The dam burst. Tears ran down her wrinkled face. Manny made no attempt to wipe them away.

How would she survive on silent conversations with Piggy? How would she survive without his flirting, never missing a chance to make her feel wanted? How would she survive without him sitting next to her, holding her hand, drawing away to make her green tea?

That reminded her that she had skipped her morning tea. She had felt neither hungry nor thirsty since Piggy's demise. But she had promised Piggy that she would continue to celebrate life, as they had learned to do together. And Piggy had promised to wait for her on the other side, until they were reunited.

'Oh Piggy, why did you have to go,' she moaned.

Manny made her way to the kitchen. Without realising what she was doing, she made a cup of Piggy's favourite long black coffee with cold milk. Only when she was pouring the beverage did the fragrance hit her and she realised what she had just done. Once again, she could not hold back her tears.

Will I ever learn to live without him? She wondered. She felt as if she had been on a roll these last four decades. Piggy used to call her his lioness. He had instilled in her the courage to handle life's lows, to take them in her stride. With him by her side, she had bounced back every time life had dealt her a whammy.

Manny decided to stick with the long black. She walked very slowly to the back patio where Piggy and she used to start their day. As she sat there sipping, the doorbell rang.

'That's strange,' she thought. 'Who could it be so early in the morning?'

'Mum, where are you?'

Manny smiled beside herself.

It was Erika, her daughter from her previous marriage. Erika, her husband John and their children Gavin and Belinda.

The children hugged her tight.

'Oh that feels so good,' said Manny.

Erika smiled. John looked relieved to see her relax.

3

Erika and John were a happy, well-adjusted couple, much like Piggy and Manny had been. They ran a successful business.

Having done their bit, Gavin and Belinda ran off to play.

Manny led Erika and John to the patio.

'I'll make you tea,' she said.

Erika nodded. She seemed to think it was good for her mother to do things. She followed her mother to the kitchen. Manny carried her long black with her, sipping it as she readied the tea tray.

'Ma, you're drinking coffee pa-style? Missing him, huh?'

Manny felt no shame in front of Erika. Her moist eyes met Erika's. She nodded.

That was enough to set off Erika. Even though Erika had not been Piggy's biological child, he had loved her dearly. In fact, Piggy had always been more possessive about Erika than Manny.

Erika cried with her mother. She had loved Piggy more than just as a father figure. He was her best friend and a mentor too. He had stood like a brick beside her through thick and thin.

Erika had been nine when Manny and she had relocated from India. Erika could never forget Gulshan attending to their every need throughout the journey, making sure that they were comfortable from the moment that Manny decided to walk out of her marriage.

Erika had always been fond of 'Uncle Gulshan' as she used to call him, and so, when Manny had told her that henceforth they would be living with him, she hadn't felt unnerved.

When the time came for Manny and Erika to step out of her previous marital home, Gulshan had been there to take them away. Standing outside a rented car, Gulshan had held out a hand to Erika, and said, more than asked, 'Friends, beautiful?'

Erika's face had lit up, 'Yes', she had replied, as she shook his hand.

Erika could never forget that. Neither could Manny. With Piggy's support, Erika had blossomed from a shy child into an educated, confident woman. She would be fifty the following weekend.

Piggy had made extravagant arrangements for her fiftieth birthday, Erika knew. She wanted to cancel the event. She was in no mood to celebrate when she was mourning the loss of a man she had loved so much. She brought up the topic when they were back on the patio.

'Mum, I'll call the caterers and all. Let's just have a quiet day.'

'No, Erika. Let's go ahead with the dinner. It's what he would have wanted.'

'But mum...'

Erika simply couldn't understand her mother's attitude.

'Trust me, Erika,' said Manny, her voice almost a whisper.

Erika blinked back more tears, trying to be strong for her mother's sake.

'Okay', she said.

When it was time for Erika's family to leave, Manny opened a drawer that Piggy had never allowed her anywhere near when he had been alive. She knew that it was stuffed with Gavin and Belinda's favourite sweets and chocolates. He would regularly replenish the drawer for his grandchildren.

Despite his advanced age, Piggy had been great friends with Gavin and Belinda. The three used to play together.

Seeing Piggy giggle with the young ones had made Manny love him even more... if that was possible. She had fallen head over heels in love with her lion the very first time they had met.

Gavin and Belinda got twice their usual quota that day.

After Erika left, Manny decided to take a nap. She didn't feel like doing anything. She was struggling, struggling to live without Piggy. Every moment seemed to stretch into eternity whereas with Piggy, time would fly.

Slipping into bed, Manny became aware that the quilt smelt of Piggy. She wondered how she could hold onto that. She tossed and turned trying to get some sleep.

It didn't work.

Eventually, Manny dragged herself out of bed. She forced herself to eat some fruit.

She wandered around the house in a daze for most of the day. She opened Gulshan's cupboard and breathed deep, trying to get a whiff of him. She thought she was going crazy.

When she finally hit the bed, she did something she had never thought she would need to do. She popped a tranquilizer. She badly needed to switch off.

October 31, 2069

'Good morning, Piggy, it's six AM.'

Gulshan's alarm woke up Manny with a start.

It was programmed to say more.

'You're waking up on a chilly morning. It's 5 degrees Celsius now. Today's high will be a chilly 8 degrees Celsius.'

Just hearing the temperature sent a chill down Manny's spine. Winter was early that year. She was used to waking up in Piggy's arms, not alone in a double bed.

Piggy knew that Manny couldn't stand the cold. He would slip out of bed to turn on the heater about half an hour before her usual waking up time. Having done that, he would slip back into bed and draw her into his arms.

Today was different. Piggy wasn't by her side. It hit her. He would never be by her side again.

'I don't want to live alone, Piggy, I miss you,' she sobbed.

With no incentive to get up, Manny stayed in bed.

The clock showed 08:37 when the doorbell rang. Manny wasn't asleep, she was just lying in bed thinking of Piggy.

She walked slowly to the door. It was Nikki, her daughter with Gulshan. The precious life they had created. They had doted on her from the very day Manny had gotten to know that she was pregnant.

Nikki had been holidaying overseas when Gulshan had passed. She had cut short her stay and rushed back on the first flight she got.

Nikki hugged her mother tight on the threshold. Both broke down.

Nikki and Manny were still holding each other on the doorstep when a car drove up. It was Erika. She had brought Manny's favourite croissants from a nearby bakery. Gulshan used to bring some for her every day.

Erika and Nikki were not just step sisters but the best of the friends. They hugged each other.

'Aren't you feeling cold standing here?' asked Erika, and continued, 'Gosh, mum, you're beginning to turn blue. Let's get inside, quick.'

They walked in. Nikki wheeled in two bags.

'Let's take mum back to bed,' suggested Erika. 'I'll get some tea, mum you haven't had tea as yet, have you?' she asked.

Manny shook her head. She gladly allowed Nikki to help her back into bed. Nikki went round to Gulshan's side and slipped under the covers.

Nikki propped herself up in bed so she could face Manny. She gently stroked back a loose strand of Manny's.

'Mum, how are you?'

Manny blinked back tears.

'I guess I'm alright,' she whispered.

Nikki shook her head. 'Of course you're not,' she said. 'How could you be, so soon?'

Erika entered with the tea tray and the croissants and some other goodies piled high on a plate.

'What are you chatting about?' she asked.

'I was just asking mum how she's feeling,' explained Nikki.

'Ah!' said Erika. 'How would anyone feel after losing the love of their life after nearly fifty years?'

Erika looked at Manny and smiled. Manny smiled back through her tears.

'Dad was pure love, mum. He would die for you anytime, anywhere, and probably for us too. He loved us so much. His passing will be hard on all of us.'

'I miss dad. I wish I could bring him back. Why did he have to go so far away that we can't be around him?' chipped in Nikki.

Gulshan had doted on Manny and his daughters. He could never see tears in Manny's or his daughters' eyes. He just couldn't handle seeing them upset. His family was his weakness.

He had always wanted to spend all his time with Manny and his daughters, so much so that he had taken a decision to stop working when he brought Manny from India.

'I've made enough money to live well and raise my children,' he would say. 'I don't want to accumulate more money.'

If anyone asked him what his best asset was, his eyes would glow with pride and he would proudly say, 'Manny, my love, my life, and my daughters. I couldn't have asked for anything more.'

Nikki looked thoughtful. She was lying down now. Erika was sitting at the end of the bed, legs drawn up, partially under the cover. They all looked very cosy.

'Mum, 47 years is a hell of a long time,' said Nikki.

Manny nodded. She took a deep breath.

'And you knew dad even before that, right?' she asked.

'Yes,' Manny replied.

'Hmm.'

Nikki looked as though she wanted to ask something.

The girls knew that Gulshan had been Manny's second husband. Of course, they also knew that they were step sisters. Manny and Gulshan had explained their situation to the girls as soon as they were old enough to understand. Especially Erika.

Gulshan had been very clear that he wanted Erika to know why her mother had chosen to leave her biological father in India to marry Gulshan. Manny vividly remembered Gulshan talking to Erika.

'Sometimes, husbands and wives don't get along, sweetie,' he had said. 'They might live together but they don't enjoy each other's company. Your mum and your dad were somewhat like that.'

Erika had been nine when Manny and Gulshan had started to live together.

'Oh!' she had said. She had looked as if she still didn't understand.

'I met your mum at a dinner and we became friends,' Gulshan had continued. 'We ended up loving each other very much.'

Manny had let Gulshan take the lead in that conversation. She sat by to answer any questions Erika might put to her.

Erika had turned to her mother and asked.

'Do you miss my dad?'

Manny had answered honestly.

'No, Erika. I never have. Look, leaving him wasn't an easy decision. I kept Gulshan waiting forever. It must have been difficult for him.'

Manny had looked at Gulshan with great tenderness at that point.

Erika had caught the loving look. She had always felt great love between her parents, and it made her feel comfortable.

'Erika, I chose to leave your father because we had no relationship except a marriage certificate. I had a piece of paper on the one side, and Piggy on the other.'

Erika had smiled at that.

Manny remembered how she had craved Gulshan's company ever since they met.

'You were quite young then, Erika,' Manny had continued. 'But as you grew, my distance from your dad would have become evident to you, and it would have made you uncomfortable.'

Manny remembered when she was still dithering over whether or not to walk out on her former husband, Gulshan had asked her what sort of an example she was setting for her daughter. She and her husband had been sleeping in separate rooms for years. They had had no intimacy.

'Mums and dads should hug each other, right, Erika?' Gulshan had butted in.

Erika had nodded in a cute way.

'Well, there you go then. Your mum and your dad had a problem. They never used to hug each other.'

Manny had smiled at that. Trust Gulshan to put it simply. He had a way with words and shared such a great bond with Erika.

Manny felt so grateful for the life they had built. She felt good for having pulled Erika out of a dictatorial household, for that, indeed, was what her former marital home had been. She had never had the freedom to do whatever she wanted to do, whenever she wanted to do. She felt gratitude to Gulshan, her Piggy, for helping her to overcome fear and feel courageous enough to walk out with him. To think that so much good came into her life because she had a moment of awakening, a moment of satori all those years ago.

Manny's deep thoughts were interrupted when Erika put her hand on her shoulder on seeing her mother smiling.

'A penny for your thoughts, mum,' she said.

'Just happy despite missing him,' she said. 'Happy that we had a good life together, happy for you girls, you had a good father.'

Manny's eyes reflected pride and happiness even though they were tinged with sadness.

Erika and Nikki were comforted to see their mother show early signs of acceptance. It was the first step to moving on.

'We're proud of dad too,' said Nikki. 'We're blessed to be his daughters, mum.'

It was time for Erika to go to work. Manny felt more alive by then. She and Nikki saw off Erika.

Nikki, after such a long journey, was completely knackered. She retired to bed.

Manny went back to her bedroom. It was where she had spent most of her life with Gulshan. It looked the same. Just Gulshan was missing. There was no one to hug, no one to chat to. She reached out to the top right drawer of the chest that she had selected for him. It held all his accessories. She ran her hands over his pens, bracelets, collar inserts, and cuff links. She smiled to see one bracelet meticulously perched on satin padding in a box. She had gifted it to Gulshan in 2017. She felt tears welling up in her eyes. Just then, she saw an envelope peeping from under the trinkets. It read "For the love of my life". Her heart pounded as she picked it up and opened the envelope.

Manny shook open the piece of paper. Two photographs fell into her hand. One showed Gulshan and her at a dinner. That was the first time they met. The other was recent, from an overnight stay at a seaside resort. Including the photographs with the letter was his way of telling her they had shared such a long journey. Including happy shots were his way of telling Manny that she made him happy.

The letter was dated October 17, 2069.

The Last Letter

Hey Beautiful,

I miss you already.

Oh please, stop crying. You promised you wouldn't. At least, you promised you would try not to cry when I'm gone. Baby, it's time to keep your promise.

I was thinking, my love, I'm still around you. As long as I'm in your heart, I haven't gone anywhere.

I'm so glad that we got to spend your birthday together. I've always considered it my most special day. The day my love came into this world has to be the best day of all.

I'm so glad I could kiss you one more time. My love, I could keep kissing you forever. Gosh, don't I sound like a crazy, infatuated teen?

I'm not, my love, I've been crazy about you since we first met. What I feel for you is no infatuation. It runs deep. As I write this letter to you today, I'm feeling emotional because I know this is it. This is my last letter to you, baby. My time has come. But before I go, I need to say a few things. So sit back and listen to me my love, my espresso. And don't bloody cry and don't butt in. Let me win this round even though, you know, I always prefer to lose to you, because the smile on your face when you win is divine.

Thank you for all you've done for me. Thank you for accepting my love and accepting me into your life. Thank you for loving me. Thank you for helping me experience life.

You know, baby, I've never been able to figure out the best moment of my life. Was it the first time I saw you, or our first date, or our first kiss, or the first time we made love, or when you decided to spend your life with me, or when you left India to live with me. Every moment spent with you has been better than the last.

Remember the first time you came over to my place for dinner? It was love at first sight for me. I can never forget how much we laughed. I couldn't sleep that night. I kept tossing and turning, and then pacing my room. I wanted to be around you. I wanted to have you around me. I just couldn't get to sleep. I could hardly wait for the morning to contact you.

And then you being you, you delayed responding. You played with me from the start baby!

Slowly and gradually, 'us' unfolded, and with that, I felt as if my life was just beginning. I started living with you, baby.

Whether it was our hidden coffee dates, our first kiss, the first time we made love. I have lived every moment since I got to know you. You have been a blessing, nothing short of divinity peppered with fun and camaraderie.

Remember the first time you treated me like your punching bag? Sure, sometimes you were tough to handle but I felt that I had finally arrived. I knew you shared that comfort level only with your closest loved ones.

Remember when I got calls during our love making? When mum would be standing outside the house with her friend waiting to come in? Those were crazy moments. I'm laughing as I write this.

Remember how we used to argue like lawyers in courts? You hated acknowledging I was right. The 'real' lawyer in you could not accept it.

You know, I'm wearing the black leather jacket you got me from your overseas trip in 2017. It's threadbare but I couldn't care less. It's been my saviour many times. In the early days when we couldn't be together all the time, I would wear it whenever I felt low. I'd feel you were around. That's just one of the ways in which you kept me going, my lioness.

When the going was tough, you started calling me "my lion". And I would literally roar for you. You made sure I walked with pride.

Since we met, there's never been a day that I've not woken up with you or thinking about you. For me, my love, you've been my world. You're all I needed. You complete my soul. You complete my instinct for companionship. Seriously, babe, you are the sexiest woman on the planet. I just need to see you to feel the urge.

Ever since we met, I became the richest person in the world. Your laughter, your touch, your kiss, your eyes, your smile and the way your eyes light up when you're happy, I'm the only one who sees all of that. No one could be richer than me.

I hope I've never let you down baby? I hope you think you made the right decision to walk away from a life of darkness into the light? All I ever wanted was to put a smile on your face. I did my best and I'm sorry if I failed in any way. If I end up leaving the world without fulfilling some of your wishes, know that I am waiting for you on the other side and will make it up to you.

Thank you for giving me Erika and Nikki. Thank you for being such a great mum. Thank you for bringing them up so well. They're beautiful women but not a patch on their mother. You're the most beautiful (in and out) human I know on this planet.

Look after our girls. Erika will be sadder than Nikki. Reach out to her. They're special. They've had a good life so far and I'm sure they will continue to have a great journey.

Sorry for one thing, my love. Sorry for leaving you alone. My heart feels heavy just thinking of how you'll manage without me. Just this one time, I'll let you down. Forgive me. It's not my doing. It's certainly not how I wanted our love story to end... I guess it had to be this way. I could never have handled seeing you leave. I haven't a clue about what lies ahead but I promise to wait for you ... as long as it takes.

I'm leaving behind a diary. It's in the bottom drawer of my clothes chest towards the back. It contains stuff I wanted to share with you but never did. Don't ask me why. I guess some confessions are hard to make in person. Life's like that.

I think you'll enjoy reading it. You'll relive some good moments and some not-so-nice-ones, just like I did while writing.

We did it my lioness, my love. Thank you for walking by my side. I could never have asked for more.

Hugs, my love, and here's a kiss, on your forehead.

I love you Manny, my baby.

Till we meet again.

Yours only,

Gulshan, Piggy, Your Lion

PS

Sorry for the blotches, the dried up tears. I can't control myself. I was never a cry baby but the thought of leaving you makes me weepy. Now you'll realise why I've been so emotional all these days.

Manny gasped for air. She found it hard to breathe. She always thought she knew how much Piggy loved her but this was overwhelming. She desperately wanted Piggy back so that she could wake up in his arms and relive life. Alas! There was no turning back the clock.

November 1, 2069

Deep in slumber, Manny felt a set of arms hugging her. Vaguely, she thought, 'it can't be Piggy, then who?'

She tried to stir herself but she felt so sleepy from not having slept much the previous few nights. Last night perhaps knowing that Nikki was sleeping in the adjacent room she slept better.

'Mum, you're cold to touch. How are you feeling?'

It was Nikki.

She had come to check on Manny and had felt that something was not right.

Manny realised that she was feeling cold despite being under a duvet. In fact, her body was shivering. Nikki had only just switched on the heater. Her throat felt sore.

'I'm fine, Nikki,' she said. Her voice sounded so throaty that Nikki looked worried.

'Should we call Dr Smith?'

'Of course not, I'll be fine after I have some tea.'

'I'll get it right away, mum, you just stay in bed,' said Nikki, not sounding convinced.

As Nikki left, Manny looked around the room. She could feel Piggy's presence.

'Good morning, Piggy! I hope you're doing better than I am,' she thought rather than said aloud.

Feeling exhausted even without getting up, she flopped back into bed.

Nikki walked in with tea and biscotti.

Manny's eyes grew moist to see the tea tray set exactly like Piggy would have laid it out.

'Biscotti, Nikki?'

Nikki smiled. She knew that Manny loved biscotti.

'You lead the way, mum. You need to eat. I'll follow you.'

'Dad introduced you to biscotti, didn't he?' asked Nikki.

'Yes,' said Manny, 'while we were courting.'

'That must have been fun,' said Nikki. She wanted to make her mother talk rather than bottle up her thoughts and feelings.

'It was,' Manny reminisced. 'He would always buy biscotti during our dates. He would split the biscotti in two, one for me and one for himself.'

'After we got married, he would always give me the first bite.'

'I'm going to have half the biscotti,' she said.

'Sure, mum.'

Manny broke the biscotti into two halves. She closed her eyes and imagined Gulshan was having his half.

She opened her eyes to see only her biscotti half on the plate.

'What the...' she started to say when she caught Nikki's smiling face and saw that she was chewing something.

'You cheeky girl...' she said, and smiled in spite of her sadness.

'Come on! Finish your half, mum. Dad commanded me to help you finish it!'

Manny obediently finished her half.

When she saw her mother take the last gulp of tea, Nikki asked, 'Game for a walk, mum?'

'Huh?'

'I said a walk, mum. You haven't been out of the house since dad left.'

It had been more than a week since Manny had gone for a morning walk or meditated. She hadn't felt like doing anything. But this was different. She would have Nikki's company. Not wanting to let down her daughter, she said, 'Okay.'

'Great. I'll go pull on some warm clothes. You too,' said Nikki.

Manny went to her bathroom to get ready. Piggy's track pants and jacket were hanging next to hers. They used to walk together every morning. She remembered how Piggy would flirt with her every morning. Piggy's love for Manny had kept her young. He could never have enough of her. He would wake up every morning with gratitude for another day with Manny. Their bodies had grown old but his love for his wife was still young. When their eyes locked, which would happen very frequently, you could literally see the deep connection between the two. Theirs was a love story beyond the material realm.

It was a sunny day with very little traffic.

Nikki knew her parents' beat. She steered her mother on the same route.

Manny felt a bit listless. She walked slowly.

'Mum, are you feeling tired?' asked Nikki.

'No, why do you ask?'

'The spring is missing from your step,' observed Nikki.

Every turn on the road reminded her of Gulshan. They would walk holding hands, Piggy on the traffic side to protect his beloved wife. His aunt had died young in his childhood, hit by a two-wheeler while walking on the road. As they walked, they would talk about anything and everything.

A few minutes later, Manny had had enough. 'Let's go home,' she said.

'Okay.'

'Are you hungry, Nikki?'

'A bit,' she confessed. 'And you?'

'A bit,' said Manny.

They smiled at one another.

Manny went straight to the kitchen to make breakfast for Nikki and herself. She peeped into the fruit basket. The avocados had turned black and mushy.

'Hmm,' she thought. Gulshan had always bought fruit for just a couple of days, always ripe fruit.

She decided on egg on toast and coffee for breakfast.

Manny honestly had a little appetite. The fresh air had done her good. But when it came to eating, she struggled. She could feel a lump at the back of her throat. It made swallowing practically impossible.

'What's the matter, mum?'

Manny looked at Nikki rather helplessly, saying nothing. It was the first time she had sat down for breakfast after Gulshan died. How was Nikki to know? She had only got in the previous day.

'Perhaps you should take a muscle relaxant,' suggested Nikki.

'I'll try an apple,' said Manny.

Manny managed to eat half an apple. At least she managed to gulp down the coffee.

It had been more than four decades since Manny had last experienced a deep sense of loss. She had lost her father a few years before she left India to be with Gulshan. She had loved her father more than anyone. He had encouraged her to study law. He was her biggest champion before she met Gulshan.

Manny had never had the courage to tell her father about the sorry state of her marriage. If she had, he would surely have pulled her out of that household.

Manny had once gingerly told her mother about her situation but her mother had asked her to try to adjust to the situation.

Manny had grown up in an affluent, fairly modern family. When she was younger, she had always heard her paternal and maternal grandmothers and some elderly ladies talk about how a woman's husband's home is her ultimate destination. A point of no return, if you will, because once a woman is betrothed, she is as though her husband's property.

Manny knew all of that. She just thought that if a relationship didn't work out well for a woman, then, surely societal norms would offer her some respite?

Apparently, a woman was meant to suffer.

Manny's love life had gotten off to a bad start. In her late teens, she had been let down by her boyfriend, who she had loved immensely. She was gutted when she found out that he had cheated on her. She had still not recovered from that heartbreak when her parents had accepted a marriage offer from the family of a young man who was besotted with Manny.

Manny's in-laws were an affluent family living in the same city. Her parents were convinced that it was a good match. She would have every comfort of life. Harpreet, her husband, was employed in the family business. As for whether his mindset matched Manny's, well, that wasn't something her family gave much consideration to. They expected Manny to "adjust" to her husband's whims and fancies. He was interested in her, and they thought that should have been enough for her.

It took Manny just a few months to figure out that her marriage was a big mistake. The family treated women (well, all the women in the family except for the matriarch, Manny's mother-in-law) like property. Manny had to ask for permission to step out of the house, no matter for what reason—to meet friends or to visit her parents. Her in-laws placed a lot of emphasis on keeping up with the Joneses. Their life was a whirlwind of social dos. Intimate family moments were a no-no. In that family, no one connected one-on-one. Manny didn't see eye-to-eye with her husband on any subject. Her love life was a disaster. Harpreet treated her like a mannequin when they made love, caring little for her needs, leaving her feeling used every time they had sex.

If anything could be worse, in the early years, Harpreet was physically abusive. Manny walked out of their home when she felt too traumatised. She spent ten months away from him, mostly with a sister overseas. She was happier there. Then "well-wishers" convinced her parents to patch up things between the estranged young couple. Manny reluctantly came back to her husband. The only change was he no longer raised a hand on her.

Manny felt like a bird living in a golden cage—a cage where she had every material comfort but no freedom, a cage where she had relationships but no love, a cage where she had a beautiful bed but no peaceful sleep. How badly she wanted to fly away... but it seemed impossible. How could she walk out of the marriage when no one was willing to help her resettle?

In a few years time, Manny had a daughter—Erika. When Erika was a baby, Manny had shifted to a separate bedroom because Erika would wake up every night feeling hungry and cry until she was fed. The idea was not to inconvenience Harpreet. But Manny soon felt a sense of relief from being away from him. She ended up staying in the separate room.

Harpreet didn't complain. Manny wondered if he was having an affair with someone. Probably yes. She didn't have the slightest inclination to find out.

'As long as I don't have to succumb to him,' she thought.

After that, Manny grew distant from her husband. Sure, she would still dress up for every social do and talk intelligently with guests as her husband and in-laws expected her to do. For the world and her in-laws, she was the trophy wife her husband wanted so he could show her off to society.

Behind the scenes, however, Manny grew increasingly depressed. Occasionally, she would need an extra glass of wine to sleep. She also felt great disinterest in meeting anyone. Except for the time she was engaged with Erika, she felt as though she were dead.

Sitting at the table across Nikki, Manny remembered those years when she had been miserable. Then out of the blue, a sliver of light had entered her life.

She recalled the evening when her family was going over to Gulshan's place for dinner, and she was told to get ready. She was least interested, as always, but had no choice but to comply.

She remembered being introduced to Gulshan, thinking that his eyes twinkled so, liking his smiley face. But not giving him more thought after that until he approached her and started to chat. And that was it.

She remembered laughing at an anecdote he shared with her. And then him laughing about something she shared. She remembered how she had then looked at him almost wondrously. How could someone change her mood just like that? In the space of an hour, she had gone from feeling dead to feeling alive. She had felt very attracted to Gulshan's intense eyes and humour.

In the week thereafter, Manny had received an invitation to meet up again from Gulshan.

Manny knew that it would be tricky to manage but she so wanted to spend time with him. She accepted thinking she would manage to sneak out somehow.

Over tea and biscotti, Gulshan had coffee and biscotti, Manny shared her life story with Gulshan. He was saddened to hear about her living conditions.

Gulshan was a great proponent of freedom and respect. He believed that everyone should have the freedom to follow their path, to achieve their heart's desire. Manny's suppressed situation and the toxic environment she was living in were the antithesis of how he believed every human should live.

Neither Manny nor Gulshan were looking for a relationship but who can deny love when it comes knocking at your door?

The bird in the golden cage, after what seemed like an eternity, had found a partner to fly with. Gulshan, like an eagle, would wait patiently within eyesight of the cage. Whenever the bird was uncaged, she would fly to the eagle. Both would fly high, sometimes the bird would ride piggyback on the eagle, a beautiful sight against the azure sky.

It saddened the bird to return to the cage. The eagle's heart would sink too, and he'd feel helpless. He knew the hardships the bird would experience back in the cage. Just the thought of meeting again kept them alive.

Without fail, the bird would fly out at the first chance. Without fail, the eagle would be waiting for her. Life together was a dance. They had found their soul mate.

Love had an amazing effect on Manny. She would see her Piggy everywhere, while cooking, watching television, taking a nap, shopping, everywhere. She felt complete. She felt as if life was looking up. In time, Manny's friends and family became aware that she had changed. She was noticeably happier.

The fact that Manny had a separate bedroom meant that Gulshan and she could engage in late-night text chats and telephone calls. This they did like teenagers, pinging and texting and calling like crazy.

Manny's morning would start with Gulshan. She would wait on her balcony to see Gulshan drive past at 7am for a glimpse of his love. Even chilly and foggy mornings didn't deter them from that morning exchange. Love had happened.

In that high, Manny had thought that she could not ask for more in life. Gulshan thought differently. He wanted her to have more. He loved her so much that he wanted life's best for her. That was why he encouraged her to desire more. He made it clear that he was by her side and wanted to give her one more chance at living life.

It took Manny time but she was glad that she had been willing to take a chance. Her last four decades with Gulshan had been full of happiness, togetherness, friendship, and love. Just as Gulshan had completed Manny she had completed him. Gulshan had never experienced such love in his entire life.

A knock at the door broke Manny's trail of thoughts. It was Nikki. She had come to check on her mother.

'Dinner is ready, mum,' she said. 'I hope you can eat more than half an apple!'

Manny smiled.

'I'll try, Nikki,' she said. 'What have you made? Something nice will help my appetite grow.'

'Oh mum!' she groaned. 'How does pasta with pesto and a veggie side sound?'

Manny followed Nikki out of the room. She had planned on starting to read the diary that Gulshan had left for her. She pulled it out and put it on her bedside table. She couldn't wait to read it. She felt it would be the nearest thing to spending time with Gulshan.

For the first time, Manny ate well.

'Well done, mum,' said Nikki. 'I'll call Erika and tell her. She'll be thrilled.'

Manny smiled, stood up and stretched.

'Well, I'll leave you to call her and clear up. I need to turn in, is that okay?' she asked.

'Sure, mum. You take it easy.'

Walking into her room, Manny shut the door and turned on the lamp light. It was cold but she didn't feel it. A rush of blood in her veins kept her warm. She slipped under her quilt and picked up the diary. Her heart was beating fast. She felt anxious as she turned to page one.

The First Page of the Diary

Hi Beautiful,

I know you're feeling lousy. But hey, reading this will be fun. I promise it will cheer you up. All you have to do is follow one simple rule—read only one chapter a day and that too, before turning in.

You know, baby, I was blessed to have met you and spent a lifetime with you. In my final moments, I decided to relive some occasions that are still fresh in my mind. Some moments were joyful, others less so. But strung together they make our beautiful journey. I decided to give you a chance to relive those moments too. I may have bungled up some dates, forgive me for that.

Remember, I'm never far from you. You made a lover of me baby, now pay for it 😊. I love you so much I can't wait to have you by my side again!

Hugs and kisses,

Gulshan

GULSHAN'S DIARY

INDEX

CHAPTER ONE

My life before I met you

I grew up in a middle class family in the decade before India's economic liberalisation kicked off. Life was a struggle; it left me with no time for romance. Even after I went overseas for further studies, my monetary struggles and perhaps my reticent nature kept me from getting hitched with anyone. Not that I was averse to being in a relationship. I simply wasn't the kind of guy to look for love.

I have always believed that love just happens. For me, love isn't only about physical attributes. I believe a meeting of minds must precede a physical union. As I said, I have always believed that love just happens.

Somewhere along the way, a family we knew proposed that their daughter marry me. I knew my to-be wife's sibling, and had seen her. That was about it. I personally had no opinion of my proposed wife. I was a goody two-shoes and so, I was happy to go along with whatever my parents suggested.

But, and this is a big but, prior to my marriage I made it clear to my parents that my wife and I would live separately. Let me explain why.

During my teens, I had grown very aware to the plight of many married women in India. Many were abused or ill-treated. That depressed me. I used to wonder what's wrong with humanity. Many (or most) women were financially dependent on their husband, and had to ask their spouses for money. That annoyed me. Why should a woman have to ask for money? Why should the needs of a woman be less important than a man's? Even if they are homemakers, and especially if they are so, women should have equal and free access to a family's resources, as the men do. I wanted to treat my woman with all the love and respect she deserved, and more.

Some of my thinking was new age for my middle class background. It didn't resonate with the people around me. Even my parents didn't think like me, and so, I decided to live independently after I got married. I found, hired, and furnished an apartment before my big day.

While I had never experienced being in love before I tied the knot, I had a lot of expectations from marriage. I desired a great life partner, someone who would understand me, who I would understand. We would champion each other.

When I got married, I thought this is it, now my life is complete.

Did I make a good husband?

Try asking my first wife that question! We're divorced, so as you would imagine, you'll be told that I was a lousy partner.

My biggest marital challenge was that there were three of us in the marriage. My wife had been in a relationship before we got married. She was upright about that fact, but she also told me that it was well and truly over. The thing is it wasn't.

Manny, I didn't make love to my wife for eight long months after we were married. I needed to know that she was emotionally free before I could touch her.

I eventually did only to realise, years later because she was a pro at hiding her emotions, that she was still caught up with her former lover. Perhaps that was why we had a miserable sex life? We couldn't connect well because her mind was caught up elsewhere.

My wife didn't enjoy my company. She used to say that I was an open book and life with me was boring. That was because I used to share everything with her. I'm made that way. I'm a regular guy. I don't keep secrets from the people I love.

'There's no mystery to life with you,' my wife would say.

Relatives did their best to patch up our relationship when they got to know that things between us were going downhill. We obliged them initially but when it became impossible to continue our marriage, we went through a very bitter divorce, bitter because my wife demanded a fat alimony plus custody of our children. She got what she wanted, I hope.

I was a wreck after my marriage ended. I felt I had lost out on love. At one point I even felt I was going crazy. I actually became suicidal. I sought the help of a doctor. In all that, the one bright spot was that my in-laws stood by me, and of course, my parents and my siblings stood by me like a rock.

I felt very sad to lose my father during that low of my life. He succumbed to a heart attack precipitated by worry about my wellbeing.

Manny, during the time my divorce proceedings were underway I got into a relationship with a woman. I thought we had a connection. But you know what? When we were travelling overseas I got to know that she was cheating on me.

I was devastated. Being let down is so depressing, irrespective of whether you're a man or a woman. Some people say that men get over failed love affairs quicker than women but that's a generalised statement. I don't believe it. I had high expectations from love but after being let down twice I felt like a loser in love. I couldn't understand what I had done wrong.

They say, once bitten, twice shy. I don't think that applies to me. I've dated one woman after that. Definitely not many women as a 'free' man in my circumstances might have. I've never been able to go out with a woman unless I connected with her at some level.

But love? Love eluded me. I thought I'd had it with love for my life... until I met you. When I met you, Manny, my life changed. I was in love. I didn't try to love you. It just happened. I saw you and experienced deep love. In you, I found my soul mate. Your love put me on top of the world baby. I had never felt so loved before. You know, it's a great feeling.

Chapter Two

Our providential meeting

I read somewhere that there's no such thing as coincidence. I agree. Your coming into my life is enough proof. You didn't come into my life by coincidence but rather, as part of a master plan that entwined you, me, Erika and so many other lives.

'A great rendezvous' is how I look back on our first meeting. Even a few minutes before you entered my house, I hadn't the remotest clue that the next few hours would change my life forever. I hadn't the remotest clue that in ushering you into my home, I would also be ushering you into my heart. I hadn't the remotest clue that love and happiness lay just round the corner.

Remember these lyrics from the Beatles number, *I saw her standing there*?

...And the way she looked, was way beyond compare, so how could I dance with another, ooh, when I saw her standing there?

We didn't dance that evening but I sure lost myself the moment I first saw you standing at my front gate. How could I pay attention to another guest when your eyes, your smile and the way you held yourself, were so beautiful, so correct and were beckoning me? We talked like there was no tomorrow. We laughed as though we were the only ones in the room. My heart sank when it was time for you to leave.

When you were walking out, I felt a part of me was walking out. All I could think of was 'how do I get in touch with her'?

It may sound crazy but even then, I felt we were meant for each other.

Somehow I managed to get your number. I wanted to text you a message. But I didn't want to single you out for obvious reasons. So, I texted all the attendees a polite message asking for the opportunity to meet again. I forced myself to wait for an appropriate time to text even though waiting was the hardest thing to do.

Finally, I sent the text. And then you being you, you played with me. You took your own sweet time to reply. I remember checking my handset like every five minutes until I got your first text.

I remember running my finger over the mobile screen, over your name, caressing it in happiness. I was in the seventh heaven. My face wore a big smile as I started to type back a reply. That started a text chain. You questioned life. We had some intense, serious conversations. Before long we decided to meet over coffee. In the run up to our first date, my heart pounded faster than I have ever known. I had butterflies in my stomach, a novelty for me. All of those were signs that love had already happened to me. I was sold to you. I had become yours.

What followed in the ensuing weeks was nothing short of a miracle. A few dates later, you accepted an invitation to visit me. I made some green tea for you because by then I had gotten to know your preference, and then showed you our home before we retreated to my study.

Standing next to you, my heart was pounding and my hands were shaking. I looked down at you. You looked up at me. Our eyes locked. In one swift movement we were effortlessly drawn into each others' arms. We kissed. God knows how long the kiss lasted but it was beyond doubt the longest and sweetest of my life. Your moist lips were locked in my mouth.

It was not just physical contact between us. It was something more than that. I experienced love at a different level. I experienced something divine.

We struggled to open our eyes. I felt as though everything else in the world had blacked out. Only we existed. No, even we did not exist. We had merged into one.

I remember looking into your eyes after what seemed like eternity. I could barely see you as my eyes were teary. I was overcome by emotion. Your eyes were full too. You know, my love, starting from that first kiss, every time I have kissed you, it has always gotten better, even now that we have grown old. Sure, we don't kiss for as long. But our kiss last night took me down memory lane. I felt young, baby. You're still as magical as when we first met.

After that, we started to catch up for tea (for you) and coffee (for me) every day. It was tough for you given that you were living with extended relatives under the same roof. Still, you managed to sneak out and meet me. We always tried to meet at different cafés to avoid you being spotted with me. Occasionally, we got caught.

The weeks rolled on until it was time for me to leave India. We visited a temple the day before my flight. I felt a strong urge to solemnise our relationship then and there, baby. But I couldn't.

That night, I cried my heart out. The thought that I would see you one more time, and then that was it, chilled my heart. I so badly wanted you to travel with me. But you had already made it clear that you didn't want to deprive Erika of her father's love. If you separated and took Erika away from her dad, you felt Erika would be upset with you when she grew up.

I cried to see our love being sacrificed. I felt helpless. I would have done anything to help you get out of your situation. I would have done anything to make 'us' happen.

I said bye to you with a happy face. I didn't want to burden you with my pain. I felt that would be unfair when I had said, 'I understand', when you explained your position.

I found it hard to stay composed during the flight. The air crew asked me a couple of times if I was okay. They must have been surprised to see a grown man sobbing.

The day I left India was one of the saddest days of my life.

CHAPTER THREE

When distance became our biggest challenge

We talked every day after I got back to Australia. We shared everything with each other. We whispered sweet nothings to each other. We expressed the desire to sleep hugging each other and wake up in each other's arms.

I used every term of endearment for you. You sometimes sent me links to love songs, making my heart dance with joy. I felt your love and it gave me hope. Hope that our love would eventually win and one day, you and Erika would join me.

Remember when I bought our first home?

We were so excited and you said that you'd do it up. I window shopped, catalogue shopped and showed you the possibilities, and you told me what to buy and place where. We still have some of those bits of furniture.

We used to speak to each other for a couple of hours daily but as the months rolled on, I realised why long distance relationships are tough to keep alive. My need for physical contact grew. I wanted to smell your hair, look into your eyes and go for long walks with my arm around your waist. I wanted to tell you that the distance between us was wearing me out but I felt you might think I was putting pressure on you to change your decision so I kept quiet.

You were so sweet. You were there whenever I faced a low. You'd call me your lion and that made me feel strong. How can a lion show himself to be weak in front of his lioness? I'd put on a brave front again. But soon enough, the emptiness within would start gnawing my heart again.

I managed a quick visit to India. During our morning chats over many cups of tea and coffee, I dropped a few hints about getting together.

'Manny, I'm willing to relocate anywhere in the world to be with you,' I said. 'You just choose the place.'

'I'm sorry,' you said. 'I've told you before that I can't walk out.'

Then you said, 'Piggy, why don't you settle down? You need someone by your side 24x7.'

How could you have said that, Manny?

I hadn't been with another woman in all the time we were separated. I couldn't. I didn't feel like seeing anyone.

When I got back home after that visit, I started to write stories and poems to help you understand how I felt. You loved what I said but you stayed firm on your stance.

I started to see a shrink. I thought that it would help me get over the depression that was affecting my moods and energy levels. I remember those sessions in her clinic. I would cry and cry shamelessly, giving vent to my pain. In the first few sessions, the psychologist encouraged me to express my feelings.

'You've got so much pent up inside,' she would say. 'Let it out.'

I felt I had failed. I couldn't understand why love wasn't a good enough reason for you to decide to live with me. Why hadn't my love and willingness to do anything to make you happy won you over?

During one session the psychologist said, 'You're in love, Gulshan. Are you aware of that? Have you accepted that emotion? Are you fighting it? Or is your love not being reciprocated?'

I nodded when she asked that last question.

Then she gently asked, 'If there is no chance of your love being reciprocated, might it be worthwhile for you to withdraw from a relationship that seems to be damaging your psyche?'

I tried to tell her that you had social compulsions to live by and that I couldn't imagine life without you and so I was in a bind.

I stopped visiting the psychologist after that. It made no sense because I was unwilling to do what she was suggesting.

Then Covid-19 struck. If I had to identify a single event not of our making that triggered the lowest point of our relationship, it would be the pandemic. Crazy travel bans meant that I was stuck down under. You lost your father. I so wanted to travel to India to be by your side, but I couldn't. Erika's school instituted a new online learning routine which ate into our time together. How could I object to that? My work suffered. I needed to spend more time during the day to push contracts. You felt I was busy when you had snatches of free time. Yes, baby, but work was important too. My only workplace goal was to establish a business that would generate enough passive income to indulge you and our daughters (yes, daughters, I always wanted to create a beautiful life with you). I never ever spent any time that I could have chatted with you doing anything other than work, and certainly never socialising. You were my world.

Sure, we continued to chat. But having less time to spend together made us crabby. We started to snap at each other for petty reasons.

India's first Covid-wave abated and domestic travel picked up. You told me Harpreet was taking you and Erika for a holiday. We wouldn't be able to speak for a few days but we could continue to chat.

'I understand,' I said. But I was jealous, so jealous. I wished that I was in Harpreet's shoes. I wanted to live with you, eat with you, sleep with you, go to the movies with you, walk with you, talk to you...

I joined a gym to help me focus. No matter how painful the gym sessions were, it wasn't a patch on the pain of separation.

Then one day you told me you were feeling guilty.

'What are you feeling guilty about?' I asked.

You didn't say anything. You asked me not to call you for a few days. I respected that. When we spoke after a week, you said family matters had kept you busy. But you also said 'I'm sorry,' and you confessed that you had cried a lot during those days because you had missed me.

On the one hand, I felt a sense of relief that you were still mine. On the other, I had a gut feeling that something was amiss.

I asked you again, 'What was in your mind when you said that you were feeling guilty?'

'I was feeling guilty about cheating on my husband,' you said.

Your words hit me hard. I couldn't fathom why someone who had no relationship to speak of with her husband would feel guilty about loving me. I felt a crack in our togetherness. For the first time since we had been together I experienced doubt. I wasn't sure if you wanted to be with me or not. I wasn't sure if 'us' would ever become a reality.

I felt desperate to tell you how I had felt in the last couple of years. I felt desperate to tell you what you meant to me. I wanted you to hear me out for an hour but you weren't willing to give me that much time.

I remembered the psychiatrist I used to visit. I wondered if giving you a break would help shake you to your senses, make you see what you were losing.

Eventually, I messaged you saying I don't want to be a side dish and would rather have you take your time and come to me whenever you were ready. I said I would wait.

That message went down very badly, you got very agitated. I couldn't understand your response. There I was facing denial upon denial and still wanting to find a way to win you over, and there were you with an open offer to take your time and come back to me when you were ready, and that piqued you.

For the first time since we had come together, I felt that I was losing the game.

Instead of saying sorry, which is what I was feeling, the man in me, insecure and shaken to see his world crumbling, made the situation worse by asking, 'Are you seeing someone else?'

My heart didn't believe that could be true. I had always felt love in your voice, even in your sadness, in your distance. I had always trusted every word that you spoke. But the devil in me wondered whether you were seeing someone else, and so, I asked the question.

You were shocked. You didn't reply for a long time. Finally you said, 'Yes, I am', and quickly followed that up with, 'Don't call me again, okay.'

'Yes, I am', you said but your voice suggested that you meant 'No. Are you f***ing out of your mind?'

'How could you, Manny, how could you?' I asked despite reading the truth between the lines.

My crazy self thought that your answer explained why you had grown distant in the last few months.

'I've been cheated,' I thought.

I was so wrong.

We were both suffering the ill effects of a long distance relationship. But at that moment, I saw red. I wanted you to feel some of the pain I had carried since so long. So I used some pretty harsh language. You got even more upset. You never could handle anger. It made you clam up, withdraw behind a protective wall.

'Don't call me again,' you repeated, and disconnected.

I felt devastated to hear you say so.

In the following days my heart and head had a tiff. My heart insisted that I hadn't been cheated, as my head believed. Eventually, my heart won hands down. All those thoughts of having been cheated fizzled in the face of my love for you.

I began to think of ways to make amends. You weren't contactable. You had blocked me. I tried to reach you via Harpreet. That went down even worse.

I realised that there was only one way to salvage us, and that was, face to face contact. I would have to travel to India. But I couldn't because of the travel ban.

The world felt like a jail. I was imprisoned in a country thousands of miles away from you. I was ready to give up everything to be with you, to save our love. How could I reach you?

All my life, I have never lacked the courage to handle challenges. It simply isn't me to twiddle my thumbs and wonder what to do next. So despite hitting rock bottom, my mind was firm about finding a way to climb out of the well.

'I'll put all my energy into finding a way to circumvent the travel ban,' I thought. 'There has to be some loophole.'

I committed to myself that I would reach you before your birthday. As you very well know, I made it.

CHAPTER FOUR

Bringing Erika onboard

Manny, I was remembering the time when you broke the news of your impending separation to Erika.

Do you remember how it happened? We were sitting in a café when you said, 'How do I tell Erika about us?'

'I've spoken to a child psychologist,' I said.

Hearing that, you looked worried. 'What if the person gets to know who you were asking for?' you said.

'Manny, calm down,' I said. 'The psychologist isn't in India. She's very good in her work. She specialises in counselling children whose parents are getting divorced or already are. I chose someone overseas for confidentiality.'

That calmed you down a bit.

'What did she say?' you asked.

'She said Erika's line of thinking will be very focused on the little things that make up her life, such as, will she still be able to play with Kareena, her friend who lives down the road? Will it be difficult to make new friends in her new surroundings? Such stuff,' I explained.

'She said one of the most important things is to let the child know that the divorce is not happening because of her,' I continued. 'It's better to say that mum and dad have decided that it is better for mum to move out.'

You started to look stressed again.

'But what reason can I give her? She'll never understand why I'm moving out.'

'True, she's too young to understand,' I had said. 'But there are ways around that.'

'Like what?' you asked.

'Like telling her that mum and dad aren't close the way mummies and daddies usually are, and so, they have decided to live separately,' I said.

You looked as if you didn't understand what I was getting at.

'You know her friend Kareena,' I said.

'Yes.'

'When I came over to your place the other day, she walked in with Kareena and the two were giggling about something. I heard Kareena asking Erika, "Haven't you ever seen your dad kiss your mum?"'

'What?' you said, sounding shocked. 'When was this?'

'I just told you Manny this was a few days ago.'

'Erika said nothing to me,' you said.

'Manny, what would you expect her to say to you?' I reasoned. 'She was engaged in girly talk with her peer, a close friend. That's absolutely normal. Children don't tell their parents everything.'

'Hmm,' you said. 'What did Erika say to Kareena? Did you overhear that too?'

'Yes,' I said. 'Erika said, "No I haven't."'

'Look, I've been telling you for close to two years now that Erika will realise at some point, soon, that her parents have an abnormal relationship,' I said. 'It'll make her uncomfortable. But hopefully, she will not get to that point, right?'

You nodded.

'So you just need to tell her that you and her dad have been finding it hard to stay together like mummies and daddies do, and so you have decided to live separately.'

'This is so hard,' you said. 'If this is hard, how will I ever tell her about us?'

'It'll happen, step by step,' I said. 'Are we ready to rock and roll?'

You smiled weakly.

'Come on, woman, you're looking as if you're sitting for an exam or something.'

You laughed.

'That's better,' I said.

*

I asked you to let me hear your conversation with Erika.

'Why do you want to listen in?' you asked.

'I'm not a spectator in all this, Manny, I'm offering to father Erika,' I said, as gently as I could because I knew that that was a touchy subject.

A few hours later you did as I'd requested. Erika and you were sitting in your room, Erika was doing her homework.

'Sweetie,' you said.

48

'Yes mum,' said Erika.

'I need to tell you something,' you said.

'What?'

'Have you heard of the word divorce?' you asked.

'Yes,' said Erika. 'Dad told me about it when we were watching a movie.'

'Oh?' you said, somewhat taken aback. 'I had no idea.'

Erika just shrugged her little shoulders, you told me later. We laughed at her attitude.

'What did you want to say?' asked Erika.

'I'm planning to divorce your dad,' you blurted out.

My love, your words sounded tactless to me, I was listening very carefully. I was especially interested in the impact of your words on Erika.

You were both silent for a long time.

I could only imagine what Erika's face was looking like. Finally, I heard Erika ask 'Is it because you guys don't kiss?'

Despite the seriousness of the situation it took all of my efforts to prevent myself from laughing. I was dying to hear your reply. In my mind I thought, 'Manny, your daughter is far more intelligent than you think.'

'I guess,' you said.

'So who'll look after me?' asked Erika.

I could then understand what the counsellor I spoke to had meant when she said that children are more concerned about day-to-day living than the philosophical right and wrong aspects of spousal separation.

'I will,' you said.

'Did dad say that?' asked Erika.

'Yes, he did, actually,' you said.

'Who'll look after dad?' she asked.

'Dad's a big guy,' you said. 'He'll look after himself.'

'So you're reeaalllly going to get divorced?' asked Erika.

'Yes,' you said.

'Where will we live?' asked the little one.

'I'm figuring that out,' you said.

'Will I be able to play with Kareena?' asked Erika. 'What about school? I will go to the same school, right? Will I get to meet dad?'

'I'm figuring that out too,' you said.

Later you told me that Erika had looked at you dubiously. Clearly, she wasn't impressed. She wanted answers and she was displeased when you couldn't answer. And then came the best part, 'If you need help figuring all of that out, maybe you should ask Uncle Gulshan for help,' she had said.

Once again, it took me a lot of effort to prevent myself from laughing out loud. I was so proud of Erika. I thought she was a super cool child.

'Erika,' you said. 'Why should I ask Uncle Gulshan?'

'Because he knows about stuff,' said Erika.

You wondered where that was coming from.

'Like he knows how to cook and stuff,' said Erika.

'Right,' you said, finally beginning to relax. 'I'll consider your suggestion, sweetie.'

'So when are you getting divorced?' asked Erika.

'Soon,' you said. 'I need to talk to your dad.'

'Erika, I don't want you telling anyone what I just told you, okay?' you added. 'It's a secret between us for now.'

'Okkkay,' said Erika.

I could tell from Erika's voice that she was struggling with that instruction. 'She must want to tell Kareena,' I thought.

'You finish your homework, sweetie,' you said. 'I'll go take a shower.'

You disconnected the call.

'Manny, thank you for letting me listen in,' I texted you.

*

We had decided that I would visit your home the next morning on the pretext of cooking breakfast. I was well acquainted with your in-laws; that's how your family came over to my place for dinner the evening we met. So my coming over for a social visit was perfectly acceptable. I was going to show you how to make penne pasta with tomato sauce.

'Hi Erika,' I said when she opened the door.

'Hello Uncle Gulshan,' said Erika enthusiastically.

'Shall we head straight to the kitchen?' I asked.

'Sure thing,' she said.

You joined us on the way.

'Hi, I managed to get all the ingredients except the goat's cheese,' you said.

I smiled, and held up a bag. 'Don't worry,' I said. 'I figured you might find that difficult so brought some to be on the safe side.'

'Wow!' said Erika. 'See mum, I told you Uncle Gulshan is great at figuring out things.'

'Yes, sweetie,' you said.

'So...' said Erika meaningfully.

It seemed obvious that she wanted you to tell me about your divorce.

I thought I had a great opportunity to talk about the subject with Erika. The previous day, I felt that you had failed Erika in being unable to answer all her questions.

'Children ask for a lot of practical details,' the counsellor had told me. 'The better you can answer their questions, the more comfortable they feel about the situation.'

That was why I had wanted you to give Erika the whole picture in one shot, about moving out of your present home and leaving India. But you had felt uneasy about the whole discussion and wanted to do it in stages.

'What's up Erika, Manny,' I said.

By then we were in the kitchen and I had started to demonstrate how to make the tomato sauce.

'Mum...' prodded Erika. She seemed adamant.

You took her cue.

'You see, I'm thinking of divorcing my husband,' you started to say.

'Oh!' I said, trying hard to look surprised. 'Why's that?'

'You know we haven't been spending much time together and we don't think alike on most things,' you said.

I nodded. 'Yes, I know you guys have had a rough time,' I said.

Erika was listening very closely.

'So you think it's a good idea for mum to get divorced, Uncle Gulshan?' she asked.

'If your mum feels that she needs to move on, she must,' I said. 'Does it scare you?'

'No-oh,' said Erika, 'just that I asked her about school and where we would we live and she didn't know.'

'Oh!' I said.

Turning to Manny, I said, 'If I can be of any help, do let me know. I would even be very happy to help you and Erika settle in Australia where we have some excellent schools.'

Erika's face lit up.

'Really?' she said, her voice oozing excitement.

'Why not,' I said. 'Manny, what do you think?'

You saw how I had skilfully steered the conversation in the direction we wanted. You realised that at that moment I needed your stamp of approval. You looked at Erika and asked, 'Would you like that, Erika? Should we take Uncle's help to resettle in Australia?'

'Yes!' said Erika, excitedly.

'Super,' I said, 'then that's settled.' I looked at you meaningfully.

'So have you ladies been paying attention to what I've been doing on the kitchen counter?' I asked in a light voice. 'We've made the tomato sauce and I'm now putting water to boil to cook the pasta...'

We spent the rest of the hour happily readying the penne pasta in tomato sauce.

Chapter Five

Life down under

2022 was a very special year. Erika and you accompanied me to Australia. It was hard to tell who was more excited on the way. You, me, or Erika. It was a big move for you and a huge change of life circumstances for me.

I had made a commitment to myself that life would be fun from the word go. One of your comments that had touched me deeply was you saying that you dreaded weekends.

'Why's that,' I had asked you, very curious.

'My husband's home at the weekends and so are the other men in the family,' you had said.

'So?' I had prodded. 'How is their being home scary?'

Up until then I had yet to understand the full impact of your relationship with your husband on your psyche.

When you opened up about weekends being scary, I realised how much you were missing out on life. You as well as Erika because there was no way a sensitive child like Erika wouldn't pick up her mother's vibe and emotions.

'Everyone's in their room, and so I have to walk on tiptoe to get around the house,' you said. 'A lot of rooms are out of bounds because the littlest sound will disturb them.'

'Oh', I said. 'So they don't believe in ice-cream Sundays, huh?'

'No, of course not,' you said with a wry smile.

'Okay,' I had said, making a mental note then and there that I would rectify the situation for you when we were together.

*

Back to 2022. There were so many firsts for you and Erika, and I was delighted to show you around.

Do you remember our first drive Manny?

We saw so much wild life. I can never forget Erika's shrieks of happiness.

We drove by the sea as well as inland. We visited the beach. I encouraged Erika to swim in the ocean, and we got in together, egging you on to join us. You didn't but Erika got a taste of the ocean, and boy, how she liked it. She showed herself to be a real water baby.

What was most important was the impact of all this family time on you and Erika.

How you used to laugh at Erika's and my pranks. You always thought that we were crazy and maybe we were. For the first time in my life I had a family I loved and who loved me.

I remember Erika's comments on one of these outings, 'Uncle Gulshan, this is so much fun,' she said. 'Will we always have fun like this?'

'We sure will, baby,' I said.

'But we never went out with daddy in India,' she said.

I didn't want to give daddy a bad name when he was no longer a part of our lives. All I said was, 'Life's different in this country, baby,' I explained.

'Mummy knows, she's been to UK and the US, families in those countries and in Australia live for the weekends.'

'Really,' Erika said, in wonder.

'Yes,' I said. 'People are very outgoing, they enjoy a whole lot of outdoor activities. Swimming, cycling, hiking, dancing, drives along the coast, visits to the beach and of course, heaps of sports like tennis, cricket, soccer and others, there's just so much to do.'

'Here, entire families play sports together,' I continued. 'It's family bonding time. If they need an instructor, so be it. They all learn together.'

'In India it wasn't like that,' Erika said.

'No baby, India is different,' I said. 'I've seen families bonding over a wedding in India, but never over physical activity. It's always children play with children, and few elders play anything at all.'

'Here, people don't think only of earning money,' I said. 'Do you understand why people work baby?'

'Yeah,' said Erika. 'You need money to buy stuff.'

'True,' I said. 'But tell me, how much stuff does a person need?'

Erika looked thoughtful.

'I guess you need some clothes and some books and some food and a house and a car and a tennis racquet...' she said.

I burst out laughing. That stopped her.

'Sorry baby,' I said. 'Please carry on.'

'And I guess other stuff,' she said.

'Okay' I said. 'So you're okay with one car, not two cars?'

'Yes,' she said. 'But mummy should have a car whenever she needs one.'

'Of course,' I agreed.

'So in Australia, baby, you'll see most families have money for all the things you just listed, but they may not have money to keep say, 3 to 4 cars,' I explained. 'They spend less time working and more time with their family. So daddies come home earlier from work than you have seen in India. Does that sound okay?'

'Yes,' said Erika. 'It sounds awesome.'

'Great,' I said. 'So now you'll understand why I have time for you even on a weekday.'

'But Uncle Gulshan, are you sure that you have money for all that stuff?' she asked.

I heard concern in her voice. I wanted to end that there and then.

'Yes, baby,' I said, in my most confident voice. 'We will always have money for the things you spoke of.'

*

In our early years in Australia Erika and I never gave a name to our relationship. It would have been too weird.

I was in no hurry to be called 'dad'. For me, I'd assumed that mantle the day you walked out of your in-laws' home. Remember? We got home and settled Erika in. Later that evening I sat you down and handed over the paperwork for deposits in your name and in Erika's name. I had made a

57

commitment that I would provide for her and I intended to live up to my commitment.

I continued to be Uncle Gulshan for a few years until a ballet dance recital. Erika was sold on learning ballet and I was happy to indulge her. I went alone for that recital because you were pregnant. I went to meet Erika backstage. She stood with a friend.

'You were stunning,' I said.

Her friend asked, 'Is that your dad?'

Erika looked at me and smiled mischievously. 'Yes,' she said. 'Yes, he's my dad.'

I smiled from ear to ear.

Erika had known that we were a couple from a few days after you walked out. We sat her down and explained that to her and she was very receptive. Until we did that, we were cautious to maintain a distance and sleep separately.

But I had never wanted to pressure her to call me dad. It would happen in good time, I thought. That day, after the dance recital, it finally happened.

*

They say that time is a great healer and indeed, our experience with our extended family showed that it is.

Two years into our life together we hosted your sister and her husband from the UK. You had thought that their stay would be awkward but it turned out to be just fine.

She was gracious towards me and I left no stone unturned to roll out the best hospitality to her.

We did the usual lunches and dinners and drives and concerts that you do with guests. The best evening however was the one before they left.

She and I sat on our patio with a pot of coffee.

We weren't engaged in a discussion or anything but at one point, she said, 'Gulshan, I must thank you for what you've done to Manny.'

I looked at her and smiled.

'Whatever I've done for Manny has been my privilege,' I said. 'I'm grateful she accepted me.'

'I'm sure,' she said. 'You're both so happy together; we're happy to see you. And my word, Erika was always a smart child but how she has blossomed.'

'Mother is also happy for Manny,' she said. 'She may not say it over a call, that's only because of the distance and her age. But mother is also very happy that her daughter has found happiness.'

I bowed my head.

'Do you think mother would want to meet Manny?' I asked.

'Yes,' she said. 'Yes, she would. Not just Manny but all three of you. You're family. She wants to meet you.'

I'm glad that we made it to India the following year.

Remember our stay? Your mother couldn't have been warmer, she fussed over us and Erika and we had a whale of a time.

That's how life should always be, Manny. Happy.

Chapter Six

Erika got a companion!

Manny, you're the most beautiful woman I've ever seen. I'm the luckiest man in the world for having spent my life with you, for having loved you, and for having created a life with you.

I will never forget the first time we spoke about creating a life together. It was back in India. I gently asked you if you would consider creating a life with me.

'Well, I always wanted two children,' you said, with a smile.

I was thrilled.

'If the baby is a girl I'll call her Nikki,' I said.

You continued to smile indulgently.

I love children. I love innocence. I love growth. I love the way you can steer the development of a young mind.

A few years later you made me the happiest man in the world when you told me that you were expecting a baby. Our baby.

I held you in my arms and stroked your hair.

'Thank you,' I said.

Remember how Erika squealed with joy when we told her about the baby. She was thrilled to bits.

'So will I have a baby sister or a baby brother?' she kept asking, until we got fed up of telling her we hadn't a clue.

We used to burst into laughter just thinking of the times to come. I felt like our family was weeks away from being complete.

In India, we would never have been told the gender of our unborn baby but Australia fortunately had no such rule (and no son preference). So, at your second ante-natal sonography we got to know that we were having a baby girl. My heart leapt with joy.

I saw you looking at me in the clinic. You weren't sure what my reaction would be although I had confessed to you the previous night that I badly wanted a daughter.

'We'll call her Nikki,' I had said, reiterating something I had said years before.

'Why Nikki?' you asked.

'Nikki means small in Punjabi, our mother tongue,' I said. 'She'll be our little one.'

You just smiled. You were happy to let me have my way.

'Also, Nikki will go down well with English-speaking people,' I added, with a laugh. 'It has less chance of being mutilated.'

You smiled in amusement.

Erika was tickled pink when she saw the sonography images.

'This is her?' she kept saying. 'This is my sister?'

She kept turning the images around trying to make sense of the black and white. 'It doesn't look like a baby at all.'

'Chill sweetie,' I said. 'It's an image that tells us that you're going to have a baby sister and that she's healthy.'

'Oh! Okay,' said Erika.

*

Over the next few months you suffered morning sickness and exhaustion. Erika and I did everything possible to make your life easier. I was and will always be eternally grateful to you for carrying a life I jointly created.

I wanted the best possible care for you. We visited the best obstetric unit in the city. We explored various birthing options. I wanted to be by your side when she came.

When the time drew closer, I didn't feel like leaving you alone for even a single moment lest you needed to rush. Finally, the day came when we welcomed our daughter into this world.

I'll never forget my first look of Nikki.

She was a blob of pink, the healthiest baby that ever was, with the deepest, most piercing eyes I've ever seen. She looked straight into my soul.

I felt so grateful to the universe for having given me such a precious gift. I turned to you and said, 'I can't thank you enough for Nikki.'

You were exhausted after the long labour but I thought (and the nurses agreed) that you looked radiant.

I didn't feel like leaving you and Nikki but I needed to pick up Erika from school.

'I'll be back soon,' I said. 'Watch over her. I don't want to miss anything.'

You laughed.

'What could you possibly miss in an hour?' you said.

'Sweetheart, I've waited years for this moment, seriously, I don't want to miss any milestone,' I said. 'Be back soon,' I shouted as I ran out.

Erika came running out of her school gate towards me.

'Dad, what does she look like?' cried my excited elder daughter. 'I can't wait to see her.'

'Hmm, I think she looks a little bit like mum and a little bit like me,' I said.

'Dad, you're just kidding,' said Erika.

'Oh no, I'm not,' I bantered.

'Dad driver faster,' said Erika.

'Calm down baby, we'll get there soon,' I said.

'Dad, I'm no longer the baby,' said Erika.

'Oh come on, you'll always be my baby, my first baby,' I said. 'Erika, don't ever forget that.'

Erika smiled happily.

We had prepared Erika to welcome the little one. She was 11. Two years had passed since you had left India. The child psychologist we consulted told us that by that age, as long as she was secure in our love and involved with the care of the baby, there would be no issues of jealousy towards the little one.

Erika refused to hold my hand as we walked down the corridor to your room. She ran ahead and without knocking dashed in only to find you nursing Nikki. She was so thrilled!

What a treat for my eyes, my love. All the women I love in one photograph frame.

'May I hold Nikki?' asked Erika.

'Indeed you may,' I said.

We seated Erika on your bed and showed her how to hold the baby.

'I love her mum,' she said.

We smiled to hear Erika say so.

After about an hour the nurse came in and asked us to leave.

'So soon,' cried Erika, echoing my own feelings. The last thing we wanted to do was to leave. 'It's been a long day,' the nurse said. 'It's best for Manny if she gets some rest.'

That did it for me. I only wanted what was best for you.

Erika and I made our way home.

You were discharged the next day. I must have been the proudest father in the world. Taking Nikki home to the pink room we had specially done up for her was a once-in-a-lifetime feeling.

Manny, I've said this before but will say it again. Thank you for Nikki. Thank you for creating a life with me.

Chapter Seven

The lowest point in our relationship

In our 47 years of being together, Manny, I can pinpoint only one time when I caused you utmost grief, and until today, I feel great remorse for that.

It happened somewhere around the start of our third year of knowing each other. You asked me if I was in touch with a friend of yours by WhatsApp.

I'll be honest. I didn't like you asking me about that lady. I felt that you suspected me of having a romantic interest in her, whereas frankly, I had no feelings for the woman at all. I mean, I knew her only because of you. You had introduced us. I had interacted with her on WhatsApp, but that was about it.

I must also admit, Manny, I've been questioned a lot in my life, over my divorce proceedings, and hated it. Ever since then I carry an intense dislike for being questioned by anyone.

So, out of irritation, to cut short a conversation I saw as meaningless and to avoid confrontation, I lied to you.

'Yes, I am in touch with her,' I had said. 'But we don't interact much, maybe once in six months.'

What I didn't know then was that you knew that I had been chatting with the lady in question every few weeks. Oh, the chats were benign, absolutely harmless, there was nothing incriminating in our exchange. Just that I had been interacting more frequently than I had let on.

But the fact was I lied to you. In doing so, I caused our relationship great damage, as I would gradually find out.

When I lied, your faith in me was broken, but naturally. If I'd been in your position, I probably would have felt the same way.

When your faith in someone is shaken, your behaviour towards them changes; you're no longer able to connect closely.

In the months after I lied, you became withdrawn. You were deeply hurt by my response but you never let on. You hid your hurt very well.

I was stupid enough to miss making the connection between our conversation about the WhatsApp chats and your change of mood. It happened very gradually. Probably that's why I missed out.

How much we suffered, not just you, but us, all because of my gaffe.

I wondered if you had stopped loving me, and if so, why? I wondered if you were having an affair with someone else. I wondered if you were feeling guilty about your husband. I simply couldn't understand what had gone wrong between us. I couldn't understand what I had done wrong.

We grew distant all because of one lie.

Imagine how I felt the evening you opened up about carrying that pain all that time.

'Remember me asking you about connecting with so-and-so over WhatsApp?' you said.

'Yes,' I said, 'I remember.'

I wondered what was coming next.

'I'd seen your WhatsApp chats,' you said. 'You know what? You were chatting every few weeks and not once in six months as you mentioned.'

I was cornered, I admit.

When I realised what I had done, I felt lousy about lying. I remember saying sorry over and over again and asking you how I could make amends.

'I need time,' you said.

Of course, time is a great healer.

But I didn't want to rely on time alone. I felt miserable for having f***** up.

I did whatever one does to put things right. I continued to do things to make you happy. I made it clear that I would never ever evade a question again or answer short.

In a moment of quietude, I felt as if I had seen the light. I understood why you had withdrawn from me. Some missing bits and pieces of our love story became clear. Of course you would react the way you did. I deserved no less.

But Manny, please don't ever think that I cheated on you. It's a stretch to call it cheating even though I know that's how you saw it. I slipped up big-time, I agree.

Somewhere along the way, the scales must have tipped in my favour again because you eventually chose to walk with me.

Since then, Manny, tell me, have I ever let you down?

They say that you should never need to be with someone, you should want to be with them. Manny, after I met you, I only wanted to be with you. I craved a companionship that I only found with you. I'm so glad 'we' happened. I'm so grateful we got a second chance, an opportunity to grow stronger. I'm a very happy one-woman man.

CHAPTER EIGHT

Thank you for walking with me

John Denver's first ever recorded song was *For Baby (For Bobbie)*, a number inspired by a girl he had loved and dated.

Manny, I don't want to sound cheesy but I'd like to dedicate those lyrics to you...

I'll walk in the rain by your side, I'll cling to the warmth of your hand, I'll do anything to keep you satisfied, I'll love you more than anybody can...

And the wind will whisper your name to me, little birds will sing along in time, leaves will bow down when you walk by, and morning bells will chime...

I'll be there when you're feeling down, to kiss away the tears if you cry, I'll share with you all the happiness I've found, a reflection of the love in your eyes...

And I'll sing you the songs of the rainbow, a whisper of the joy that is mine, and leaves will bow down when you walk by, and morning bells will chime.

*

Manny, I'd like to thank you for deciding to walk by my side. I know it wasn't easy for you to get out of your bad marriage but you did, for our sake. You took your time but you chose well. Do you ever thank God for having made the right decision, Manny?

You were instrumental to keep alive an amazing love story Manny. Thank you for making me feel special. Thank you for loving me. Thank you for ignoring my flaws and for being a part of me. Nothing and no one has ever done more for my confidence than you reposing trust in me.

Thank you for choosing to live life fully, Manny. In doing so, you gave yourself a chance to be you, and you know what? You make the world a better place, a brighter place. I'm so grateful for having lived with you.

Thank you for these last 40 years, Manny. Every moment spent with you has been true bliss. You're the most beautiful woman in the world and my best friend.

You, me, Erika, and Nikki have lived the best possible life. I had the most wonderful family life thanks to you. I'm sure you would agree? I'm sure you're as grateful for the good life we've enjoyed. I'm sure you're proud of how far we've come, and our girls!

Above all, thank you for being my partner, Manny. I couldn't have asked for more. I love you.

*

Manny put down the diary in a very thoughtful mood. It was over. She had nothing left to look forward to.

'Goodness, what will I do every evening?'

Reading the diary had been a surreal experience. She had been reading, that is so, but in truth, she had felt as if Gulshan was speaking.

'Who'll tell me a story tomorrow?'

The thought that she would no longer hear his voice troubled her. A deep sense of anxiety started to come over her. Her throat choked up. She put her hand to her throat as though to unclasp the vicelike grip she could feel but it refused to quell. She started to feel out of breath, her heart started pounding. She tried to get hold of herself but she could feel her condition worsening by the minute. Manny could feel herself slipping away.

'Gulshan', she whispered. 'I think I'm coming to you, very, very quickly.'

A mystical smile lit up her face. She was ready to meet her love, Gulshan, on the other side. She saw a tunnel lit with bright white light and Gulshan standing at the far end, hand extended, waiting for his Manny.

Manny was dying but she was happy. Soon she would be reunited with the love of her life. She couldn't ask for anything more.

She felt no worry for Erika and Nikki. There were well settled.

The moment finally arrived. Manny felt her breath slow. Her body heaved one last time, and then she slipped away...

Manny's body lay in peace on her bed, the bed she had shared with Gulshan for 47 long years.

From up above, Gulshan and Manny kept a watch on the body. They saw Nikki enter the room with a flask of hot water for the bedside table.

They saw Nikki shake Manny, put a hand on her forehead, and try to open her mother's eyes before she broke down by the side of the bed, her head resting on her hands, which were folded in supplication. After a few minutes she rose and pulled her handset out of her pocket and called Erika to tell her what had happened. Tears streamed down her face.

Erika said something. Nikki nodded. After the call was over, Nikki stroked Manny's head, kissed her forehead, and whispered, 'I guess you're with dad, mum. You always wanted to make him happy. Love you'.

With that, Gulshan and Manny faded into a space where only love existed. No societal norms, no suppression, no judgement and no fear. Just love.

*

Loud beeps from Manny's alarm clock sounded in her room. Manny lay not in a bed in Australia but in a bed in India. She woke up in disbelief.

'What was that about?' she thought.

She had had a crazy dream, a dream in which she had spent 47 great years with Gulshan before he passed and she followed him.

Manny's eye caught the date on her electronic clock. September 24, 2021, 07:30.

Her birthday.

She didn't need to get up until about 07:45 when Erika would surface. Her husband would be served bed tea by the family maid in his room. So, she lay down to savour the morning and the beautiful thought of living a life so fully.

Manny had society and all its trappings and Erika's access to her biological father on the one side. That was her present life.

She had Gulshan, Erika, and a life of love and happiness on the other. That could be her future, if she chose so.

Four months ago she had chosen the former over the latter, in fear of the social repercussions of following her love.

She had fought with Piggy.

'And what did fighting with Piggy get me?' she thought. 'It's not like I've been happy all this time. I've been miserable.'

'Piggy's been doing everything possible to reconnect. I've been avoiding him. I thought I could live without him but can I? Do I really and truly want to forget him? Can I forget him?'

Manny realised how deeply she loved Gulshan. She realised that avoiding him hadn't changed how she felt about him one bit. She missed him. She wanted to spend time with him.

Had she chosen wrongly in May? Was that what her dream meant?

Manny was suddenly possessed by the desire to connect with Gulshan. She picked up her handset to message him.

"Contact blocked" flashed across the display.

'How could I have blocked you, how could I have caused you so much pain,' she thought, quickly unblocking him.

She texted: "I'm sorry. I'm so very sorry for avoiding you. Love you, miss you."

It was 07:45 in India.

Manny reckoned it would be just after noon in Australia.

'Gulshan should be up,' she thought. 'Perhaps he is at work.'

To her utter surprise, she got an instant reply.

'Happy birthday, beautiful, I love you more. Coffee catch-up at 12:30, okay?'

Huh!

Coffee catch-up at 12:30 could only mean that Gulshan was in India, in town. She couldn't believe it.

Manny clumsily let go her handset. She stood straight in disbelief. Her lion was in the same city as she. He was just a few kilometres away. She wanted to go see him right away. How would she wait for five hours?

Well, at least she could call him immediately. She called him right away. Gulshan picked up on the first ring.

It was the most intense conversation they had ever had. Very few words were spoken. Gulshan had previously never been short of words when they chatted but now he was subdued. Manny could sense his hurt, she could see tears rolling down his cheeks, and his throat was evidently choking as he found it hard to speak.

Gulshan made it clear that he had left his work for her and come to India with the sole mission of resurrecting his love.

Before hanging up, they both had tears in their eyes, only now, these were tears of joy. They would be meeting in a few hours after what felt like eternity.

On her way to the café where they had chosen to meet, Manny wondered how she would feel when she came face to face with Gulshan.

She had butterflies in her stomach. What would they talk about? Would the conversation flow effortlessly like it used to? Or might he have changed?

Walking into the café, Manny actually felt her legs tremble. Her heart raced.

She looked around. Yes, there he was, sitting by the glass pane, his face oozing love, eyes twinkling. He stood up the minute he saw her. Her eyes met his as she walked over. She reached the table. They said nothing, just gazed into each others' eyes. In that sweet silence, they spoke volumes to each other. They felt each others' pain.

A waiter neared their table.

Gulshan motioned to Manny to sit down. He didn't want to attract undue attention.

'You'll have the same?' he asked.

She nodded.

'One black coffee, one green tea,' he said.

'Sure Sir.'

The waiter moved away.

Manny's hands rested on the table, seemingly holding her handset. Gulshan reached out and took them into his.

Manny felt a quiver run down her spine. It was the first time they had touched in almost three years.

Their beverages were served.

Gulshan looked at Manny meaningfully. She understood. She smiled.

'Go for a drive?' he asked.

She nodded.

They wanted some privacy.

They left in Gulshan's rented car.

Gulshan drove the car to a quiet spot and parked. He turned to her. As though by default, their hands reached out for each other. A few seconds later, they were cheek-by-cheek, in a tender embrace.

'How are you?' Manny softly asked Gulshan.

'Much better now that you're with me,' he said.

He was quieter than she remembered him.

Gulshan stroked Manny's cheek with his right hand, his left hand held her left hand. Manny closed her eyes.

Gulshan whispered in her ear, 'I've missed you like crazy, baby'.

Manny felt tears well up in her eyes and start to flow.

'It's okay, baby, I'm here now. I'm not going anywhere without you, never, ever.'

They hugged. They savoured the moment, the peace they felt in each other's arms.

Gulshan drew away to look into her eyes. Manny knew what was coming next. She was so eager to be kissed.

Manny's handset rang. Without looking at the display she silenced it.

They kissed. It would be hard to say who was hungrier. They kissed again.

Manny's phone rang once more.

This time Gulshan reached out for the handset.

The display flashed "Erika".

'You can't ignore this call. Erika comes first.'

Manny obediently took the call.

'Mum, where are you?'

'Out doing some stuff, sweetie.'

'Will you be back soon?'

'Umm, I may take an hour. Is that alright?'

'I guess.'

'Why did you call Erika?'

'I finished my math homework. May I go play with Kareena?'

Kareena was Erika's school mate who lived a couple of houses away.

'Yes, you may, if you tell daddy before you go. If he isn't home, then tell your grandmother. And wear your sneakers, no slippers.'

'Okay.'

Manny disconnected the call and looked up to see Gulshan smiling.

'How is little Erika doing? I so want to meet her.'

'She's doing good, growing up fast.'

'I hope you haven't been disciplining her too much?'

Manny just smiled.

Gulshan was very easy-going with children. He liked to get them around with love. He believed that that was the best way to draw them out.

'You have time to talk?' Gulshan asked.

Manny nodded.

Gulshan felt at peace because his world felt complete again. His faith in love had been upheld.

But there was stuff to sort out between Manny and him.

'What do you want to talk about?' Manny asked.

'About what happened between us,' said Gulshan.

'Oh!' said Manny, 'must we talk about that?'

'Yes, Manny, we must. If we don't clear the air, there might be stuff that causes friction between us again.'

'Okay,' she accepted.

'Look, first, I want to say sorry,' he started.

At that, Manny covered his mouth with her hand.

'You don't need to be sorry, I know you were upset,' she said.

Gulshan gently removed her hand from over his mouth.

'Yes, I do need to say I'm sorry, Manny,' he continued. 'I used some pretty sharp words.'

'But Manny, you must know that since I've met you, it's been just you. That's how I like it. You've grown on me, my love.'

Manny looked very slightly embarrassed.

'Come on,' she said. 'You're a free bird, it's not like you have committed to me.'

'I have, Manny, I have,' he said. 'And that's why I need a lot of time from you. When you started to avoid me, I felt insecure.'

'Manny, I-have-never-felt-so-insecure-in-all-my-life,' he said, stressing every word.

She nodded.

'May I say something,' she asked.

'Of course, love,' he said.

'I know I told you I wanted out of us,' she started to say.

Gulshan listened to her very intently.

'I was consumed by many feelings. On the one hand, I felt guilty of cheating on my husband,' she said.

'For heaven's sake, Manny, you have no relationship with him,' said Gulshan.

'True. But we're still living under the same roof. We're bringing up a child. Our daughter,' she said.

Gulshan started to look frustrated.

'Yeah, and then you told me not to contact you if you were to be hospitalised,' he said. 'How do you think that made me feel?'

'I'm sorry, Piggy. But I also did say that I would reach out to you.'

Gulshan threw up his hands as if to say, 'And would that help quell my worry?'

'I'm really sorry, Piggy, but then you asked me some crazy questions.'

'I asked you if you were seeing someone else,' he said.

'Precisely,' she said. 'What were you thinking of, Piggy?'

'You know I've had a bad time with my husband and in-laws,' she continued. 'And then you came into my life and helped bring me alive again. You know how much I love you. Why would I want to see someone else?'

'I was insecure,' he said. 'And in any case, it didn't help when you said that you were.'

'Well, I felt hurt for being asked that question,' she said. 'Gulshan, I can't walk out on my husband for Erika's sake. I said so then and am saying so now.'

'But he treats you like dirt and your in-laws treat you the same,' said Gulshan. 'They talk badly about you behind your back. You know that, right? I mean, your in-laws look down on you.'

Manny knew Gulshan was right. She could feel his frustration. But she also realised that Gulshan needed a life partner and that wasn't being fulfilled in their part-time togetherness.

'Gulshan, you deserve better.'

'So do you Manny. You deserve to be happy. And don't get into the see someone else dialogue, I've already told you how I feel.'

She nodded.

'I won't suggest that,' she said. 'But then, are you okay with a part-time lover? You did say otherwise a few months ago.'

Gulshan had texted her saying that he was only willing to continue the relationship if she opted in full time.

He had written: *I'm no longer willing to be a side dish. But I'll wait for you. The day you choose love, I'll be there. I can no longer bear the pain of seeing you living in hell. All I want is for you to be happy.*

'Hmm,' he said. 'Manny, I felt helpless when I said that. I thought I would step back to give you time to rethink.'

'I was devastated,' Manny said in a low voice.

'I know,' he said. 'That's why you clammed up. Frankly, I was struggling with loneliness. I wanted you to feel some of my pain.'

'I'm sorry,' he added.

*

Gulshan had neither been able to rest nor sleep after sending Manny that fateful message. He had walked around his flat feeling like an idiot. He had texted her on a weekend, when they had agreed that he would never call her because of the many demands on her time from her very sociable in-laws and husband. So, he had no choice but to wait for Monday morning when the men in Manny's family would leave for work.

Manny had been furious to see his call.

'Why are you calling me? Why can't you stand by your decision? You said you wanted out, right?' she had said.

'I'm sorry,' Gulshan had replied, somewhat taken aback by the severity in her voice. He sensed that things had gone too far.

'Well, that's just too bad because I don't want to talk to you now. I'm done. How could you even think that you can call me whenever you please, and switch off whenever you want? I'm not a puppet,' she had screamed.

'Manny, please talk to me just for five minutes,' he had begged. He wondered if she really was seeing someone.

Manny had hung up.

*

Manny and Gulshan both remembered the sorry event from a few months before.

'Manny, not a day has passed when I haven't regretted sending you that message,' said Gulshan.

'That's why I tried so hard to reach you.'

'Yeah!' said Manny, in a slightly scornful voice. 'Even via Harpreet.'

'What choice did I have?' retorted Gulshan.

When Manny hadn't replied, he had reached out to her through Harpreet, whom he knew. That had made her even more furious. Anyway, their stunted conversation had yielded no positive outcome.

In the ensuing weeks, Gulshan had introspected a lot. He realised how much he loved Manny. Now he said so.

'Do you realise that everything that transpired, happened because we love each other?' he asked in a gentle, low voice. 'I never quite realised when you became my world Manny.'

Manny sighed deeply but she said nothing.

'I'm sorry I hurt you,' Gulshan continued.

A deep silence ensued.

Gulshan made the first move to break the ice. He reached out to the bracelet Manny was wearing. It was a bracelet he had gifted her when he last visited India. Her eyes followed his fingers running over the bracelet.

She reached out and ran her fingers similarly on the bracelet Gulshan was wearing. She had bought it for him on his birthday.

When they looked at each other, their eyes were twinkling.

'You came back,' said Manny, her voice throaty. 'You made it for my birthday despite the Covid-19 travel ban.'

'I had to, my love,' he said, his voice equally throaty.

They fell into a tight embrace. Love had won the day. Such is the power of love. It helps ease a lot of pain.

It was time for Manny to return to the cage, her marital home. She clung to Gulshan. Neither of them wanted to let the other go. But she had to go.

'Will we catch-up again tomorrow, at the same time?' asked Gulshan.

'Yes, yes of course,' said Manny. Her voice suggested just how eager she was to spend time with Gulshan.

On the way back Manny thought about how much she and Gulshan had hurt each other. For what, she thought? Life was so short.

The last few hours had helped her realise how happy Gulshan made her. Manny thought of her life when she had decided to step away from Gulshan. She used to hang out with friends and attend lunch and dinner parties. The whirlwind of social living was like a drug that delivers a high, only to wear off soon after and leave you down in the dumps. Sure, social-dos helped distract her from the sadness of being estranged from Gulshan. But they had left her tired, and they surely didn't help her switch off at night. Thoughts about Gulshan would consume her, leaving her tossing and turning, unable to sleep. So much so that Manny had taken to wine to dull her senses and sleep. She'd never been a great consumer of wine but after her fallout with Gulshan she simply couldn't do without a few glasses in the evening.

One day Harpreet had also commented, 'What's with you? Why are you drinking so much?'

Manny wondered if his concern came from the cost of the bottles she was downing?

Manny had never felt as alive as she did when she was with Gulshan. With Gulshan, life was one big celebration. Every moment was fulfilling. Without him, she felt empty.

Manny had been very deeply hurt by Gulshan's outburst a few months ago. His anger had come like a bolt out of the blue. But now she realised that love and insecurity were behind their fallout. She was overwhelmed that Gulshan had risked his life and business for the sake of their love.

When she had put Erika to bed, Manny picked up her handset.

Gulshan had sent her many heart emoticons and the message: "You love me, I love you. We're talking again, Manny. Where does that leave us?"

Manny texted back: "I talked to mother once, about me moving out of my in-laws place."

"You did?"Gulshan replied. "You never shared that. What did she say?"

"She got upset just thinking of me doing something like that. You know how she thinks. She's worried about what people will say."

"Bah!" texted Gulshan. Manny smiled to read his reply. She could practically see him rolling his eyes in disgust.

"How many people do you know who are continuing in bad marriages simply because they are socially and/or financially insecure or for their children?" he asked.

Manny started to think.

"Well?" prompted Gulshan, somewhat impatiently.

"Quite a few, I guess," Manny texted back.

"Well, you should have pointed that out to your mother and asked her why she supports people staying sad all their lives," Gulshan replied.

Manny was feeling exhausted.

"Piggy, let's leave this discussion for another time, okay?" she suggested. "It's been a beautiful day, but a very long one. I badly need some sleep, and I'm sure you need to sleep too."

"Me? I need you, baby," he said.

Manny blushed despite the fact that there was no one to see her.

"But I see your point," he quickly continued. "You sleep now."

Manny was exhausted but she had one more thing she wanted to do before she turned in. She wanted to connect with Priya, an old school friend of hers who had relocated to Canada with her daughter a couple of years ago, after walking out on her husband. There, she had remarried. Manny had seen photographs of Priya with her new husband and her daughter. They looked like a happy family.

Manny wanted to call Priya but she didn't have her number so she logged into Facebook to look her up.

"Hi, I bet you're surprised to see my message," she texted. "I wanted to talk, if possible. Let me know please."

Manny was surprised to see her handset flashing in response.

Priya must be online, she thought. She had immediately called Manny.

'Hi Manny, it was such a pleasant surprise to see your message,' she said. 'How are you doing?'

'I'm keeping well, Priya, umm..,' Manny felt at a loss how to talk about her life.

'What's up, Manny?' asked Priya, sensing her discomfort. 'Feel free with me. Is your family okay?'

They hadn't spoken in years but still Manny felt a sense of comfort in talking with her. That's how it is with old friends, she thought. She mustered up the courage to pour out her heart.

'Priya, my marriage is a mess,' she blurted out.

'Oh!' said Priya.

'Well, I was in a relationship with this guy who cheated on me and soon after that ended, I agreed to get married to Harpreet, my husband,' Manny said. 'Harpreet had expressed an interest in me countless times. I think I was swayed by that since my confidence was at an all time low. But it was a bad decision. Harpreet and I don't see eye-to-eye on many things. We've been living like strangers since about eight years, ever since my daughter was born. I don't get along with my in-laws. Life was really bad until I met this person a few years ago.'

'He was in the city on a holiday. We fell in love but then he needed to travel back home... and then the pandemic happened and he couldn't travel back to India. But recently he made it back...' Manny paused.

'And?' prompted Priya.

'And he has asked me to live with him. He wants to take full responsibility of Erika.'

'And?' prompted Priya again.

Manny was quiet.

'Are you confused?' asked Priya.

'My heart wants to run to him but my head says no,' said Manny.

'Ah!' said Priya. 'That tends to happen. That's social-conditioning, my girl.'

'What do you mean?' asked Manny.

'Look, ever since we were young we were conditioned to believe that divorce is a bad word and divorcees, especially women, are loose people, to be shunned,' explained Priya. 'We were brought up to fear society, to prioritise adhering to social norms over our own needs. So, obviously, we feel scared to swim against the tide. And as far as women's needs and desires are concerned, we were told they aren't important. I mean, I grew up seeing my father have the last word on everything. I never saw my mother put her foot down even when she didn't like my father's choices. I thought that was how life had to be.'

'Did you feel scared to walk out on your husband?' asked Manny.

'When I first thought of it, yes, heaps,' said Priya. 'I used to think all sorts of crazy stuff. Like, what if I end up living alone? What if no man ever wants to marry me? What if a man tries to prey on me? Who will I turn to?'

'Prey on you?' asked Manny. 'I don't quite understand.'

'I've seen a lot of women who have walked out of their marriage face men, especially married men, who see them as being available for sex,' explained Priya.

'That's disgusting,' said Manny.

'Yes of course it is, and scary,' said Priya. 'It took me some time to get used to the idea.'

'What helped?' asked Manny.

'I think the thought that I was giving my daughter a great deal, a better father figure than she had had, and the freedom to grow into her own person.'

Manny went quiet again.

'Manny?' asked Priya, 'you there?'

'Yes,' said Manny. 'I was just thinking... did your daughter not get along with her father?'

'Well, she did, in the sense that she loved him very much, he gave her a lot of presents and he never spoke harshly with her. But he was hardly engaged with her life, you know. He had practically no interest in her schooling, he never attended parent-teacher meetings, and he definitely had no time or interest in her extra-curricular activities.'

'But don't very few dads do that sort of stuff, Priya?' said Manny. 'I mean, most industrialists or business men leave home early morning and get back very late at night, after their children have been put to bed. Where's the time for them to engage with their children?'

'You're right, Manny, but again, you're just describing what you've seen,' said Priya. 'Life doesn't have to be that way. It all depends on what your priorities are.'

'What's your life like now Priya?' asked Manny curiously.

'Great fun!' said Priya. 'Amar my second husband is a family man. I can't tell you what a difference that makes to life, Manny.'

'It does,' said Manny, incredulously.

'We are his world, and money is secondary,' explained Priya. 'Sure, you need money to live well but it isn't the be all and end all of our existence, you know how it is, right?'

'I guess,' said Manny.

Priya laughed. 'You don't sound very confident,' she said.

'Look, I had everything money can buy in my previous in-laws' home,' Priya continued. 'They were fine with me spending on anything that would show off their wealth, so spending on designer wear and accessories was accepted, even encouraged. They didn't expect me to lift a finger. We had more house help staff than the number of people in the house. But life was all about things and showing off and blah, blah, blah...'

'Yes, now I understand,' said Manny, 'your situation sounds very familiar.'

There was a lull in their conversation.

'Hmm, and pardon me for asking, in what way is your daughter more free now than she would have been with her biological father?' asked Manny.

'No need to feel sorry Manny,' said Priya. 'I'm happy to help.'

'In my previous marriage, I had no freedom,' Priya continued. 'To continue my previous example about spending, if I wanted to spend on say, helping a street urchin, I couldn't. If I wanted to work, I couldn't. I had to ask for permission to leave the house, and declare where I wanted to go and why. It was plain ridiculous, like living in the Middle Ages. If I had continued to live with my in-laws, Tanya, my daughter, would have subconsciously internalised that situation as normal. I didn't want that for Tanya.'

'What about you, Priya?' asked Manny. 'In what way are you better off now?'

'Huh! My life has undergone a 180 degrees turn,' said Priya. 'What can I say?'

'Let me put it this way, Manny, my two husbands are like chalk and cheese,' continued Priya. 'I had a loveless first marriage. My husband and I couldn't connect. We had different outlooks on everything, so we would end up bickering. It was like that from day one.'

'It was an arranged marriage, right?' asked Manny.

'Yes. I think he married me for my physical attributes, you know, his family was looking for a trophy wife to show off,' said Priya.

'I can relate to that,' said Manny.

Manny could relate to most of what Priya was saying. 'How did your marriage affect you?' she asked.

'I felt suffocated all the time,' said Priya. 'I got depressed. I started to suffer from insomnia.'

'You didn't want to consider a divorce earlier than it happened?' asked Manny.

'You bet I did,' said Priya. 'I talked to my parents about walking out of the marriage but got no support from them. That just made me more depressed. I told you I was too scared to walk out without support. I was very clear that I wanted to take Tanya with me, I mean, I was practically living for her, she kept me going. But I had no confidence in my own ability to look after her, you know, from the financial angle.'

'I understand,' said Manny.

Again, there was a lull in their conversation.

Manny wanted to ask Priya if she and Amar had become lovers while Priya was still married. She wondered if that was too personal a question to ask.

As if on cue, Priya steered the chat in that direction. 'Thank God I met Amar around that time,' she said.

'How did you meet?' Manny asked.

Priya laughed. 'Believe it or not, we met in a counsellor's clinic,' she said. 'So here's the story. Amar's sister was having problems with her husband. She needed help. I was seeing the same counsellor. One day he had come to pick up his sister. My appointment was after hers. We met in the counsellor's waiting room. I was leafing through a magazine when he struck up a conversation.'

'And then,' prompted Manny.

'After a couple of such meetings, he asked me out,' said Priya. 'But there was nothing romantic between us then, you know. We just enjoyed each other's company. I felt I had found a like-minded person to chat with. The last thing on my mind was having an affair.'

'A few months passed that way,' she continued. I stopped seeing the counsellor. But Amar became a confidante. It wasn't love at first sight for us, Manny. We grew into best of friends. Amar used to joke that if I ever wanted to run away and needed entry into Canada, he'd be happy to enter into a contractual marriage with me.'

'Goodness,' said Manny.

'Yes! Amar's a scream,' said Priya. 'He takes life lightly, he says no one is going to get out of it alive, so you might as well live light and travel light.'

'Then Amar went back to Canada, but we stayed in touch. He visited again a few months later, and went back. The next time he visited, I was at an all time low. My in-laws would make it a point to show me down. That's the time we drew even closer because he sensed I was near breaking point. He offered to stand by me if I walked out of my marriage.'

'You never doubted his support?' asked Manny.

'Very momentarily I wondered if I was jumping from the frying pan into the fire. But I quickly reasoned that Amar had shown himself to be so different to my first husband that it was unfair to even think that way.'

'Were you ever worried about what people will say?' asked Manny.

Priya sounded thoughtful. 'Somewhat, I guess. But not too much because I knew I was moving away.'

'Did the thought of moving to Canada scare you?' asked Manny.

'No,' said Priya. 'That was the easiest. I felt grateful for the opportunity to make a fresh start in a new place.'

'Walking out of my first marriage was the best decision of my life,' Priya continued. 'Tanya got a great father and a closely knit family. I got a wonderful friend and husband. We have a baby girl, by the way. She's just a month old. I haven't posted her photographs on Facebook as yet.'

'Oh, that's super, congratulations!' said Manny. 'And your family is okay with your decision now?'

'They've all come around now,' clarified Priya. 'In the months after I walked out they had to face a lot of societal flak, but then living in that world is their choice. You know in India, if a marriage fails, it's always the woman's fault.'

'So there you go, Manny, I hope I have been helpful.'

'You certainly have,' said Manny. 'You've given me a lot to think about.'

Priya laughed. 'Don't think too much, Manny,' she said. 'We think with our heads whereas we feel with our hearts. I believe the heart is a better judge of what makes us happy. Ask your heart what to do.'

'But doesn't one have to be practical too?' asked Manny.

'Sure, one does, 100 per cent,' said Priya. 'But I get the feeling that your practical aspects will be taken care of, your hesitation comes from inertia.'

Manny sighed. 'Perhaps you're right,' she said.

'I don't want to sound philosophical Manny, but you know how life is, you need to give it a chance to blossom. Every seed has the potential to become a tree but how many actually manifest that potential? Very few, right? I always think that some seeds experience fear, they live and die as seeds, thereby cutting short what could have been a beautiful life.'

'You sound very wise, Priya,' said Manny.

'Oh no!' said Priya. 'I'm just sharing my feelings. It's your call, sweetie. I can only encourage you to live your life fully.'

Priya's story inspired Manny.

It was past midnight by the time Manny said bye to Priya. She badly needed some sleep. She was in a better frame of mind than she had been in the evening but she still needed to make her peace with the tag of a divorcee.

'Priya is right about the fact that my perception of divorce comes from my upbringing,' she thought.

At that moment, Manny was clear about one thing. She wanted out from the toxic life she had been living.

*

The next evening, Manny and Gulshan were sitting peacefully in a café. Gulshan was looking at her thoughtfully. He could sense that she had been doing some heavy-duty thinking.

'A penny for your thoughts?' he said.

'Been thinking about moving out of my present situation,' she said.

'Finally...' said Gulshan, with a theatrical touch. 'Happy days are round the corner.'

'Shush!' said Manny. 'I didn't say I was ready to move in with you.'

'Huh?'

'Just that I want to get out of my present situation,' Manny clarified.

'You want to go back to your family?' Gulshan asked. 'Will that be acceptable?'

'If I tell them how I've felt these last few years, I think they will collectively be supportive,' said Manny.

'Might I ask why you're not considering being with me?' asked Gulshan.

'I don't want to jump into a second marriage so quickly,' said Manny.

'Hmm,' said Gulshan.

'So you're open to a second marriage?' asked Gulshan.

Manny was quiet.

'Manny?' prompted Gulshan.

'I don't know,' she said.

'Why?'

She just shook her head in response.

Gulshan tried a different tactic.

'What are your reservations?' he asked.

'I don't want to deprive Erika of her father,' she said.

'Manny? You just said that you wanted out. And now you're saying that you don't want to move out. What's going on in your mind? What do you want?'

'Why do you ask so many questions?' she said, clearly frustrated.

'Because I love you and I'd like us to be headed in the right direction,' he replied. 'You sound confused.'

Manny didn't like Gulshan saying so even though that was probably true.

'It's easy for you,' she snapped. 'You don't have to do anything.'

'Manny I'm here to support you. I will do everything to help you get out. But you're the one with a husband and in-laws.'

Gulshan was doing his best to stay calm. Internally, he was feeling frustrated too. Manny was a tough nut to crack.

'How long does it take to get a divorce?' asked Manny.

'Divorce by mutual consent happens in 18 to 24 months,' said Gulshan. 'But there are umpteen ways to make things move much faster.'

'Look, don't worry about that,' he continued. 'Manny, we'll solemnise our relationship whenever. You and Erika can still leave India even if you're not divorced.'

Manny looked dubious.

'What's Erika getting from her father that you think I can't offer her?' asked Gulshan.

Pat came Manny's response: 'Security.'

'Manny, I've said this before and I'll say it again. I'll deposit money in a separate account in Erika's name for her to withdraw when she is 18. It'll be more than enough for her education and to settle down. She will be secure. And I'm happy to do the same for you, sweetheart, so that you're never in want, irrespective of your decision to work or sit at home.'

'Won't it be a problem to get Erika out?' she murmured.

'Are you thinking Harpreet might object?' he asked.

'Yes.'

'Why don't you broach the subject with Harpreet?' he suggested.

Manny looked at him as if he was suggesting she murder her husband.

'Come on,' he said. 'You can do it. It's not so difficult.'

'Let me think about it,' she said. 'I don't want to talk about this anymore. Change the topic.'

They spent the rest of the hour quietly. Gulshan murmured sweet nothings to her to cheer her up.

*

Gulshan called Manny later that evening. He thought he would give her a pep talk before the time when he knew she would sit down to talk to her husband. Manny took his call but spoke in a hushed voice.

'What's up?' he asked.

'We're watching a movie, I'll call you later,' she replied, and disconnected the call.

True to her word, Manny called Gulshan about two hours later.

'What was that about?' he asked.

'I told you, we were watching a movie,' she said.

'We?' asked Gulshan.

Manny was quiet.

'Who's we?' persisted Gulshan.

'Erika, Harpreet and I,' she said.

'Oh!'

Both Manny and Gulshan were quiet.

Manny broke the silence.

'Are you there?' she asked.

'Yes,' said Gulshan.

'I'm sorry,' she said. 'You sound upset.'

Gulshan didn't reply.

'Piggy?' she said.

'What?' replied Gulshan.

'What's the matter?' she asked.

'Manny, I don't get it,' he said. 'What's going on?'

'What do you mean?' she said, in a voice that suggested she was perturbed by his question.

'I don't understand you,' he said. 'You say you're mine but your behaviour suggests otherwise.'

'Why, what have I done, Gulshan?' said Manny.

'You talk about your present situation,' said Gulshan. 'You can talk for hours about your unhappy marriage, about how Harpreet doesn't respect you, about being deprived of love, about wanting out. And then you behave as if all is hunky dory with Harpreet.'

'You're saying all of this just because we watched a movie together?' said Manny.

'It's not about the movie,' said Gulshan, his voice clearly reflecting his frustration. 'It's about your choices, your future, my future, Erika's future.'

Manny was quiet.

'Manny?' Gulshan prompted.

'I'm here,' she said.

'Manny, I love you, you know that, but I don't have an endless reservoir of patience,' explained Gulshan, in a softer voice. 'I need this story to end, and I'm keeping my fingers crossed for it to have a happy ending.'

'Story?' said Manny.

'Yes, our love story,' said Gulshan.

'I want to spend the rest of my life with you,' he continued. 'I need to see this going in the right direction. Any step you take towards me is a step in the right direction...'

'I saw the movie with Harpreet for Erika's sake,' said Manny, her voice low.

'It's about your choices, Manny,' said Gulshan. 'If everything you have told me is true, about you, me, and Harpreet, then, surely you realise that you have a responsibility to me and to Harpreet?'

She said nothing.

'Don't you think Harpreet needs to get on with his life?' he asked. 'Don't you think he must miss being in a relationship?'

'He's never said so,' said Manny.

'You mean in words,' replied Gulshan. 'What about his actions?'

'I don't know...' said Manny, her voice trailing off.

'What security do you have Manny?' asked Gulshan. 'I mean, you talk about staying in your marriage to secure Erika's future but what security do you have? Are you involved with the family business?'

'I used to be but not now,' said Manny, in a low voice.

'Precisely,' said Gulshan. 'What does that say about your husband's responsibility to secure you?'

Manny looked thoughtful. Gulshan had a point.

Just recently, her in-laws had cut her out of the family business. When she mustered up the courage to ask, 'Why?' they said, 'We want to protect you from any court case that could happen.'

Huh! They had made no such move to cut out their younger daughter-in-law, her brother-in-law's wife. 'Why?' Manny asked. But she got no answer.

Effectively, their action left Manny uninvolved with her in-laws' assets, the family property, and the family business. She wasn't allowed to work. She was, she knew very well, just a trophy wife her in-laws liked to show off.

'Well,' prompted Gulshan.

'Hmm,' said Manny, cornered, but not wanting to admit it.

'Now let's talk about Erika,' said Gulshan. 'What security does she have?'

'What do you mean?' snapped Manny. 'Her father provides for her well. We may have issues but he has never denied her any gift or expense on her extra-curricular activities.'

'Say tomorrow you have a spat with Harpreet,' said Gulshan. 'Forget me. Forget us. If that were to happen, could you walk out of your home knowing that you had a bank balance to support you?'

Manny looked serious.

'No...' she said, thoughtfully. 'He gives me money every month.'

'Precisely,' said Gulshan. 'So he doles out money and he will continue to dole out money for as long as you are around. Whereas if he had a long-term view of your future, Manny, he would have either made you a joint holder of his bank accounts and/or deposited a large sum of money in your name and let you operate that.'

Manny sat quietly.

'How many fixed deposits do you have in your name, Manny?' asked Gulshan.

'Two,' said Manny.

'Is the interest from the amounts enough to cover your monthly expenses, if, say, you needed to rely on those for your income?' asked Gulshan.

'No,' said Manny.

'That's no way to treat a wife, Manny, at least it isn't in my view,' said Gulshan. 'How a husband treats his better half says a lot about what he feels for her.'

'I don't know what to say...' said Manny, before her voice trailed off.

'Don't say anything Manny,' said Gulshan. 'Look, I don't mean to stress you. Money is important. But it shouldn't become the aim of life. Money can't buy you happiness. Agree?'

'Of course,' she said.

'I mean, your in-laws are stinking rich but they don't look happy to me,' said Gulshan.

'They aren't,' agreed Manny.

'So sometime when you're sitting alone, think about security in real terms,' Gulshan suggested gently. 'Ask yourself what you can call your own without asking for permission. Know what it really means.'

'And Manny,' added Gulshan. 'Just so you know this isn't about throwing money at you but I'm willing to make these financial arrangements as soon as you move in with me, the very day you walk out on Harpreet. I simply would never want you to feel insecure even a moment because who knows what life brings.'

*

A few evenings thereafter Manny entered the café with a spring in her step. Gulshan noted her body language the minute she entered. They had spoken very briefly during the day because Manny had been busy with Erika's school routine and her exercise class. Gulshan had been in business meetings.

Gulshan waited for her to be comfortably seated before he asked. 'You'll have your usual?'

She nodded.

'One black coffee, one green tea,' he said to the waiter who was hovering around.

'Sure Sir.'

Gulshan let the boy move away before he asked, 'How was your day?'

'Good,' she said.

Gulshan was dying to know if Manny had made any progress in talking to her husband but he didn't want to prod her. Surprisingly, she spoke up very quickly.

'Guess what,' she said.

'What?' Gulshan replied. 'I don't know, you tell me."

'I spoke to my husband about leaving,' she said.

'And... what did he say?'

'I asked him if we should separate, and he said okay.'

Gulshan said nothing.

Manny looked at him as if she expected a pat on her back.

'Was there more?' finally asked Gulshan.

'Yes, I told him I wanted to move out of my in-laws home. I told him I'd go alone, and he could keep Erika.'

'What?' Gulshan spluttered, spewing coffee on the table. 'Manny, how could you have suggested that?'

He quickly took out a handkerchief and cleaned the droplets.

'How could you?' he repeated.

'But Erika is also his daughter, right?' said Manny, in a plaintive voice. 'So he has a right over her and a responsibility towards her.'

'Manny, Erika needs her mum more than she needs her dad. What does he practically do for her in any case?'

'Well...' Manny's voice trailed off.

'What did he say?' asked Gulshan.

'He said, "You take Erika and go, I'll come and live with you".'

'Huh?' said Gulshan, and threw up his hands as if to say he couldn't understand what was going on.

'What a man!' said Gulshan. 'He doesn't care about you when you live with him and yet he is so accustomed to you that he doesn't want to live without you.'

Manny said nothing.

'Huh!' said Gulshan. 'He could search the whole world but he wouldn't find someone like you who would take his nonsense.'

'Gulshan!' exclaimed Manny.

'It's true, Manny,' said Gulshan.

'Anyway,' continued Gulshan. 'At least you have the answer to your question about Erika.'

'You mean about him making a fuss if we separate and I take

Erika?' said Manny. 'Yes, that shouldn't be an issue.'

'Manny, my love, nothing will be an issue if you are clear in your mind about what you want,' said Gulshan, in all earnestness. 'You see, things will just fall into place. You just need to keep the faith.'

'Faith,' said Manny.

'Yes, Manny, faith,' said Gulshan. 'Faith in the universe, faith in your good fortune, faith in me, and faith in us...'

'You do have faith in me, don't you Manny? You do have faith that I'm not some monster who's going to gobble you up?'

Gulshan smiled.

Manny laughed nervously, 'Of course I do. Gulshan, two years ago you know I used to crave a glimpse of you.'

'Two years ago,' said Gulshan, incredulously. 'What's with the two years ago, Manny? What about now?'

Manny kept quiet.

'Manny?' Gulshan prompted.

'I love you, Gulshan,' she said.

'You sound very offhand,' said Gulshan. 'Where's your enthusiasm for life? After the way you've been treated by your in-laws, and the time we've spent together, I would have thought that you're ready to take the plunge.'

'I am ready for change,' said Manny. 'Just that... at the end of the day, maybe I shouldn't think of living with anyone until I'm comfortable with myself? What do you think, Piggy?'

'Where will you live, Manny?' replied Gulshan, trying hard to be patient. 'I mean, have you even told your family about your situation?'

Manny shook her head.

'Precisely,' said Gulshan. 'Wouldn't they find it strange if you were to just walk in one day and say you're shifting back home?'

'Actually,' continued Gulshan, 'why haven't you shared your story with your family, Manny? Family is a woman's first support.'

'I don't want to stress them,' said Manny. 'You know years ago, when Harpreet slapped me, I walked out. They supported my decision. But then when people interfered my mother asked me to give Harpreet a second chance. Now that I have Erika, I doubt they'll help me.'

'Manny, you're being unfair,' said Gulshan. 'At that time your parents were approached by so many well-wishers who wanted to help "patch" up the situation,' said Gushan. 'My parents faced the same situation when I was going through a separation. You know how relatives can be... everyone has an opinion and wants to express it and when they come together they can be pretty persuasive.'

'Well whatever,' said Manny. 'But it's hard to bring up Harpreet as a subject when he is alien to my family.'

'Alien?' said Gulshan. 'What do you mean?'

'Harpreet has nothing to do with my family,' said Manny. 'He doesn't get along with most of my relatives and hardly ever participates in family events. Actually, because of his nature it's probably good that he stays away from my people.'

'Hmm,' said Gulshan. 'Why doesn't he get along with your relatives?'

'I don't know,' said Manny.

Gulshan looked thoughtful. 'Perhaps I can guess,' he said. 'Is it because Harpreet and his family look down on your family? What about your in-laws? Do they interact with your family?'

Manny shook her head.

'Hmm,' said Gulshan. 'And correct me if I am wrong but Harpreet has never stood up for your family as he would for his own?' said Gulshan.

Manny looked disturbed. She shrugged her shoulders as if to say, 'Perhaps you're right.'

Gulshan realised he had hit the nail on the head.

Manny quickly changed the topic. 'If I told my family about my situation, I think they would see me as twice the burden I would be if I were alone,' she said.

Gulshan let the topic be changed. He had made his point, after all. 'Burden?' he said. 'What burden? I don't understand your mindset Manny. I mean, you're educated. For God's sake, how could you ever be a burden on anyone?'

'Educated but good for nothing,' said Manny. 'Come on Gulshan, it's not as if I've ever worked or have a job at present.'

'Manny, Manny, Manny,' said Gulshan, shaking his head. 'This is so wrong. You're putting yourself down. You have no reason to. Who says you couldn't get a job if you wanted to.'

'I don't know...,' Manny's voice trailed off. She sounded very doubtful of her employment prospects.

'Don't do that to yourself, Manny,' said Gulshan. 'It's unfair.'

'It's unfair to you and unfair to us,' he continued. 'If you were to move back home Manny, what would happen to us? Do you really want to postpone living?'

Manny looked at Gulshan but said nothing.

Gulshan tried a different line.

'Manny, I'd like Erika to have the best possible care. My big grouse with her life right now is that she has no engaged father figure to speak of, right?'

'Uh-huh,' is all Manny said.

'I'd like to fill that gap in her life,' said Gulshan.

'Could we travel with you if we were to walk out tomorrow?' asked Manny, taking Gulshan by surprise.

'I'm sure we can figure that out, Manny,' said Gulshan. 'I assure you that I will not leave you alone for even a second if you leave your husband for me.'

Gulshan felt he had said enough. He was quiet after that. Manny played with her empty cup and saucer.

*

Gulshan had always known himself to have an almost endless reservoir of energy. But later that same evening, he felt drained.

He lay on his bed thinking over the last few weeks. He had flown to India to resurrect his love, and while Manny appeared to still love him, her constantly wavering mind was fast sapping his energy.

He was up to facing anyone to explain his love and commitment to Manny. He could deal with any opposition so long as she stood by him. He knew how to solve any legal tangle. What he couldn't do was unravel the mind of the woman he loved. Why, when he knew where she was coming from?

Gulshan knew that Manny had tried to get out of her oppressive marriage a year after tying the knot but when that had failed, she had gotten into the habit of suppressing her emotions. About a decade had passed since those sorry events. Now perhaps she felt too jaded to opt out. What was it that she kept saying?

She didn't want to deprive Erika of her father's support.

Gulshan grunted. 'Support,' he thought. 'Huh, what does she know about children?'

He wondered how a seemingly well read woman like Manny could be so focused on the material needs of her daughter and blind to the little one's emotional needs.

On one of Gulshan's visits to Manny's in-laws a few days ago, Erika had been all over him. All because he had gifted her a tennis racquet and expressed an interest in her game.

These were some of the dialogues that Gulshan had had to deal with during the course of the evening:

'Uncle Gulshan, come and see my room.'

'Uncle Gulshan, I need to go to bed now but will you come and see me before you leave?'

'Uncle Gulshan, may I call you sometime?'

Erika had seemed so starved of love and attention. Why couldn't Manny see that? A child needed love and affection and inspiration far more than monetary support.

'Security,' is what Manny had said when Gulshan had asked her what Erika was getting from her father.

What about emotional stability?

That evening, Gulshan felt as if something died in him. He felt hurt and betrayed, betrayed by society, betrayed by Manny's fear and betrayed by what had been left unsaid. Gulshan felt he had lost his battle and for the first time in his life, he decided not to fight.

After all, fight for whom?

A woman who loved him, a woman who spoke to him a few hours every day, a woman who whispered 'I'm only yours' in his ear when they made love, and said his touch drove her crazy. But who didn't want to take him up on his offer to spend the rest of their lives together in any place in the world, and raise Erika.

Manny could continue to feel stuff and say things that didn't match her life choices. Manny could carry on a charade. But Gulshan couldn't. Gulshan wanted a life, a life with Manny and Erika. He wanted them in his life.

*

Gulshan had a very restless night. He woke up feeling more exhausted than when he had gone to sleep. In all his mental fuzziness, however, he was clear about one thing. He wanted to go back. He had come so far for Manny but she was neither willing to give herself her due nor give him his due, and certainly, she was overlooking her daughter's deepest needs.

Gulshan was sure he had given their love story his best shot. What could he do if his love was not being reciprocated? At least, Manny didn't seem willing to take their relationship to a logical conclusion.

Manny didn't call Gulshan all day. She just texted him asking: "You'll be here by 6pm?"

"Yes," he replied.

That evening Harpreet and Manny had invited Gulshan over for a meal. They sat down for a typical North Indian vegetarian meal to suit Gulshan's preference.

Manny's sister-in-law Nimisha joined them. Gulshan knew her just as he knew Harpreet and their parents.

'Hi,' said Gulshan. 'How are you doing? How's work?'

Before she could reply, Harpreet butted in. 'She's doing great,' he said. 'We're delighted to have offloaded some of our work to a trusted family member.'

Nimisha smiled at Gulshan.

Gulshan felt sickened by the family's mindset. They valued their daughter and even their other daughter-in-law but Manny was considered inconsequential when actually, Manny was savvier than Nimisha and her sister-in-law put together. They probably felt insecure when she was around, thought Gulshan, feeling very angry.

Manny had never been allowed to work despite asking so many times but it was fine for Nimisha to join the family business.

Gulshan couldn't resist the opportunity to take a dig at the family, including Manny, who he was annoyed with.

'It's great that some women, women like you,' he said, with a flourish of his hand, 'are bold enough to stand up for your rights.'

'Some women,' he continued, and here, he oh-so-delicately turned his head in Manny's direction, 'suffer in silence despite being well read and worldly.'

Manny's husband looked decidedly uncomfortable.

Manny looked worried. She seemed to be wondering what Gulshan might say next.

Gulshan then dropped a bombshell.

'I've been looking at tickets,' he said, directing his conversation to Harpreet.

Manny's ears perked up. What was he saying? Tickets? For whom?

'Oh?' said Harpreet. 'You're thinking of going back?'

'Yeah!' said Gulshan. 'Business, you know, one can't stay away forever.'

Harpreet nodded knowingly. 'Of course,' he said.

'But tickets are hard to come by,' continued Gulshan. 'The earliest seat I've been able to find is a few weeks away.'

'You'd like to travel back earlier?' Harpreet asked politely.

'Oh yes!' said Gulshan. 'I would go tomorrow if a ticket was available.'

Harpreet laughed.

'You must have very pressing business matters to sort out,' he said.

'I do,' said Gulshan, and then he made another sarcastic comment. 'To tell you the truth, I've invested in cutting-edge technology with which I can control my business from anywhere in the world. But a man needs a good reason to make a place a home.'

Manny's eyes opened wide on hearing Gulshan speak. Of course she didn't say anything just then.

An hour later, Gulshan made his way home.

When he walked out of Manny's home, he was clear in his mind that he wouldn't call her.

'I've put the ball in your court, Manny,' he thought. 'Now it's up to you.'

Manny was in no mood to budge from her stance on Erika. Gulshan could see that very well. If that were so, their relationship had no future, in which case, he was ready to bail out.

Beep. Beep.

Gulshan was still on his way home when his handset started to ring.

He glanced at the display. It was Manny. He shook his head wondrously. Now what? He took the call.

'You didn't tell me you were going back,' said a very agitated Manny.

'No, I didn't,' said Gulshan.

'Why?' said Manny.

'Why what...? Why am I going back? Or why didn't I tell you?' asked Gulshan.

'Why didn't you tell me?' said Manny. 'No, why are you going back? Okay, both things.'

Clearly, Manny was distraught.

'Perhaps the same reason holds true for both of your questions Manny,' said Gulshan. 'I'm going back because I can't carry on this way. I came for a reason and it's clear that that reason no longer holds true.'

'What?' she said. 'I don't understand Gulshan.'

Gulshan felt from Manny's voice that she was near hysterical. He decided to unload himself.

Manny, you want me as well as Harpreet,' he said. 'You want Harpreet to continue to provide for Erika. I'm not comfortable with that. I want all of you.'

'Just try to see my perspective,' said Manny, her tone now plaintive.

'What?' spluttered Gulshan. 'Oh Manny, please, I've exhausted myself trying to make you see sense. You keep harping on not wanting to separate Erika from her dad and as I've told you, her dad is her dad on paper only. He's hardly engaged with her.'

'Manny,' said Gulshan with great emotion, 'a man who dotes on his daughter wouldn't be separated from her come what may. Now tell me what response did you get when you proposed that Erika stay with her dad and you move out of the house?'

Manny was quiet.

'Tell me, Manny, why are you quiet?' prodded Gulshan.

'Didn't he say take her with you?' asked Gulshan.

Manny was still quiet.

'Manny? Are you there?'

'Yes,' she said in a sombre voice.

Gulshan had more to say.

'It sounds horrid to say so Manny, and it hurts my heart, but all you want from me is to fill a void,' said Gulshan. 'All you want is a few stolen moments.'

A deathly silence was all that Gushan got in response.

'God, I feel like the woman who sung "saving all my love for you",' he said. 'Do you remember the lyrics, Manny?'

When Manny still said nothing, Gulshan hummed a few words, 'A few stolen moments is all that we share, you've got your family and they need you there, though I've tried to resist being last on your list...'

'It hurts so much Manny, to know that I'm last on your list...' Gulshan's voice actually broke while he was saying so.

He disconnected the call.

Manny didn't call Gulshan back that night.

Gulshan slept surprisingly well, having unloaded his emotions over the course of the evening and having started the process of accepting the worst, the prospect of losing Manny.

'What the heck,' he thought. 'I came to India thinking I'd try my best to win back Manny and help her move on, but if she's happy in her hell hole, what can I do? As they say, you can take a horse to the water but you can't make it drink.'

*

Gulshan had only one plan—to go back.

He woke up the next morning feeling heart-broken but free in the sense that he wasn't going to expend more energy on Manny.

Manny, in contrast, hadn't slept a wink.

She had tossed and turned all night, thinking of what her life would be if Gulshan were to exit.

'Oh God!' she thought. 'I'll be miserable again.'

Manny recollected the previous few months when she had had no contact with Gulshan. She had taken to wine to get to sleep. She had been miserable.

Now Gulshan was in town and simply pouring out her soul to him had lifted a load from her shoulders. At least during the hours she was with him or talking to him, she felt happy, and if truth be told, that happiness was deep enough to carry her through the rest of her waking hours.

Manny covered her eyes with her palms, 'No, no, what will I do?'

She grabbed her handset to call Gulshan.

Just then Erika entered the room. 'Mum,' she said.

Manny put down her handset.

'What?'

'Mum, I want to talk to Uncle Gulshan,' said Erika.

'What!' exclaimed Manny, and then she remembered that Gulshan had told Erika that she could call him anytime.

'I don't know, sweetie, he might be busy,' said Manny.

'Mum! I'm sure he'll talk to me, he said I could call anytime,' said Erika.

'Yes, he did, didn't he?' said Manny. 'But don't you think now isn't the best time to call him.'

'No,' said Erika, in a confident voice. 'I think now is the best time to call him.'

It was quite a situation. Manny was desperate to speak with Gulshan. And she faced a daughter who was adamant to speak with him too.

Manny realised that there was no way Erika was going to let the opportunity go. Manny would have to wait for her turn.

'Okay, I'll call him,' she said.

Erika clapped her hands in glee.

'Yes!' she said.

Manny called Gulshan.

He picked up on the first ring.

'Umm, hello,' said Manny.

'Hi,' said Gulshan. It was a rare time when he didn't address Manny by the many sweet adjectives he had for her. Manny noted that. Gulshan must be very upset, she thought.

'Erika is with me,' continued Manny. 'She'd like to talk to you, if that's okay?'

'Of course it is,' said Gulshan. 'Put her on, how nice.'

Manny was somewhat surprised at the happiness and interest in Gulshan's voice. She knew that Gulshan was fond of Erika and made a special effort to reach out to the child but she had always thought that he did so for her sake. In Gulshan's voice now, she felt an interest that went beyond what she would call politeness. It was genuine.

Manny quickly pressed the speaker button. She wanted to listen in on the conversation.

'Here,' she said to Erika, handing her the handset. 'Uncle Gulshan is on the line.'

'Good morning Uncle Gulshan,' said a beaming Erika.

Gulshan could sense she was beaming even though he couldn't see the child.

'Hey baby, how lovely to hear your voice,' he said. 'How are you doing?'

'I'm very well, Uncle, do you know, I really missed meeting you yesterday,' said Erika.

Erika had gone to sleep early and hence had missed Gulshan.

'I missed you too, baby,' said Gulshan.

'Uncle Gulshan, I used my racquet for tennis practice. I did really well. You know, my coach told me that the new racquet will help me play better. I wanted to tell you.'

'Erika, I'm delighted to hear that,' said Gulshan. 'I can't wait for us to play together. I hope that happens soon.'

'I hope so too Uncle Gulshan,' said Erika.

Over the next five minutes or so Erika chatted on, blissfully unaware that every minute seemed like an hour to her mother, who was dying to get her daughter to do her homework and free her handset so that she could call Gulshan herself.

Gulshan too was in no hurry to hang up. He was genuinely enjoying his exchange with Erika. Children brought life back to the basics, he felt. The simplest emotions—love, happiness, excitement, simplicity, no wasteful thinking, no politicking, and so much more.

Finally, after Manny resorted to sign language to indicate to Erika that she had said enough, Erika said, 'Uncle Gulshan, I've got to go now, I'll call you again soon, okay?'

'Sure, baby, you call me whenever you want,' said Gulshan.

Erika disconnected the call.

Manny wasted no time in busying Erika with some books, and then she went to her bedroom to call Gulshan.

He picked up on the first ring, she noted.

'Hi,' she said.

'Hi,' answered Gulshan. 'You okay?'

'No,' said Manny. 'I had a bad night.'

'Oh!' said Gulshan. He seemed at a loss for words. That was so unlike him, thought Manny. She knew that her behaviour, actually, her decisions had brought on his behaviour. She had no clue how he would respond but she simply had to tell him how she was feeling.

'May we meet?' asked Manny.

'Of course,' he said. 'Will you come over or do you want to visit a café?'

'I'll come over,' said Manny. 'Erika has a play date with Kareena this afternoon after lunch. Would 2.30pm work?'

'Of course, Manny, see you then,' said Gulshan.

Manny disconnected the call. Gulshan hadn't called her 'my love' even once today. She sighed. If only life weren't so hard...

*

'Come on in,' said Gulshan. 'Sit down.'

Manny entered his study and flopped down on an easy chair. 'You look exhausted,' he said.

Manny shook her head. Gulshan saw her eyes well up. She tried to wipe them away. Gulshan's heart went out to her. 'Oh Manny,' he said. 'I love you so much, it's so hard to see you torture yourself this way.'

Manny started to weep. Gulshan got up and went over to her, raised her and gave her a big bear hug. She clung to him weeping.

'I love you,' she said, between snuffles.

'I love you more,' he whispered, stroking her hair. 'When will you realise that?'

'I'm so tired,' she wailed.

'Do you want to lie down?' asked Gulshan. 'Tell you what, take a nap. You're not in a hurry to get back, are you?'

'No, I have a couple of hours,' she said.

'Good,' said Gulshan, signalling the sofa-cum-bed at one end of his study.

Manny stretched out on the bed. Gulshan sat at the edge looking at her. She took his hand in hers and asked, 'Do you have work to do?'

117

'Why do you ask?' said Gulshan.

'If you don't, then lie down beside me,' said Manny.

Gulshan obediently lay down beside Manny, with his arm supporting her head, so that she could nuzzle against his chest. He stroked her hair, 'Sleep, my love,' he said.

Manny woke up an hour later to see that Gulshan had shifted to his study table where he was quietly working on his laptop.

'I slept so well,' she said.

Gulshan lifted his head and looked at her on hearing her voice.

'I don't know why I struggle to sleep at home,' continued Manny.

'You sleep well here because you feel safe and calm,' he answered.

'Huh?' said Manny. 'I'm safe at home too.'

'Physically, yes, you're safe at home too,' said Gulshan. 'But emotionally, you're vulnerable. That plays on your mind.'

Manny thought about what he had just said.

'That makes sense,' she said.

Gulshan smiled. He was pained to see Manny suffering. From the look of her, she had had a really rough night. She looked positively haggard. However, he said nothing because he felt that Manny needed to come up with her own questions and answers.

Manny sat on the sofa-cum-bed.

'A cup of tea?' offered Gulshan.

'Yes please,' she said.

She sat on the bed sipping. Gulshan sat at the desk, also with a cup.

'I hurt you,' finally said Manny.

Gulshan didn't say anything.

'But I did tell you at the outset that I wouldn't be able to give you what you wanted,' she said.

Gulshan still didn't say anything.

Manny wanted to say, 'Stay, don't go.' But how could she say that when she wasn't willing to commit to their relationship?

Gulshan could sense the tussle in her head. Still he didn't say anything. Finally, it came from Manny. 'Stay, don't go back,' she said.

Now Gulshan smiled.

'Manny, my love, I'm human,' he said. 'I'm not a hero. I'm a man. I have needs. You come and stay with me, I'll stick around forever.'

'I can't,' she said plaintively.

'You can but maybe you don't want to,' said Gulshan.

'How can you say that?' she said.

'Because your subconscious mind accepts me fully, that's why you slept so well in my company, whereas your conscious mind is cluttered with stuff from your background,' said Gulshan. 'Erika should stay with her dad and all that stuff.'

'Accept that you have a responsibility to everyone you profess to love, Manny,' said Gulshan.

'I feel I have wronged you,' she said.

'No, I'm an adult, I knew what I was getting into,' said Gulshan. 'But since you don't want a future with me, I'm getting out of this.'

'I feel uncomfortable just thinking about you not being here,' said Manny.

'Manny, the best decisions in our life are those that spread happiness. Choose wisely for yourself, for your daughter and for Harpreet,' said Gulshan. 'That's all I can say.'

'It's difficult Gulshan, when what's good for me isn't the best for my daughter,' said Manny.

'You think different things would be good for your family members, Manny, but maybe you've got it wrong?' said Gulshan. 'I believe the universe has a perfect solution for every problem, perfect because it's good for everyone involved. We're all interconnected so at the end of the day, what's good for me might be good for Harpreet too.'

Gulshan shrugged his shoulders as if to say that was all he had to add to their conversation.

Manny sipped her tea quietly after that. When she finished it, she made her way home.

*

The ensuing week was interesting.

Manny had house guests so she was caught up at home.

Gulshan busied himself with work to keep his mind sane.

What was interesting was little Erika invested a lot of time in her relationship with Uncle Gulshan. She insisted on calling him every day. Manny thought Erika was overdoing it but she was so insistent that Manny had to comply with her wishes.

Manny had another problem with Erika calling Gulshan. Erika tended to share everything with her father. While he didn't pay attention to most of her chatter, his ears would perk up when he heard that Erika had called Gulshan.

'Why is Erika phoning Gulshan?' Harpreet would then ask Manny. Manny dreaded being asked that question because she would have to concoct an answer. She really didn't know what to say.

Gulshan found it funny how at a time when he wanted to bail out of Manny and his relationship because it had no future, Erika, who was closely associated with them, and in fact, probably the reason their relationship had died, was herself helping to keep their togetherness alive.

Their talk was rather inconsequential, as you would expect from a child of eight and a grown man. However, Erika's chatter told Gulshan how much she was starved of love from a father. How could Manny have missed seeing that, he wondered? Or did she see it, and not want to accept the truth?

When Manny saw how Gulshan indulged Erika over the phone, she remembered her own close relationship with her father. She also realised that Erika's relationship with Harpreet was far from what it should have been.

Manny wondered how Gulshan would behave with Erika if he were to live with her. In Gulshan's chatter with Erika, in his concern for her, she saw shades of her own concern for her daughter. Manny was being reminded that true fatherhood wasn't so far from motherhood.

The day her guests left Manny called Gulshan and asked him if she could visit.

'Sweetie, you don't need to ask,' he said. 'When can you come?'

'This afternoon would be best,' said Manny.

'Sure,' said Gulshan.

A few hours later they sat together in Gulshan's study, a room Manny felt at home in.

'What are you reading,' she asked.

'Just some philosophical stuff,' said Gulshan with a laugh.

'Is it nice?' asked Manny.

'I enjoy it,' said Gulshan. 'I find it helps broaden my horizon.'

'Tell me about it,' said Manny.

'Oh come on, you tell me how your week went,' said Gulshan.

'No really, please tell me,' insisted Manny.

'Okay,' said Gulshan, wondering where to start.

'You know how Mahatma Gandhi said, be the change you want to see in the world?' he said.

'Yes,' she said.

'The same philosophy applies to our lives,' continued Gulshan. 'If you want something different to your present life circumstances, you need to make effort for it, and often, that effort involves changing something.'

'Hmm,' said Manny.

'I'll give you an example,' continued Gulshan. 'Consider your life. You've toed the line, done whatever your in-laws and husband expected of you, even set aside your own aspirations. Correct?'

'I guess,' said Manny.

'You're also sure that whatever Erika is experiencing with her dad is the best possible father-daughter experience she could have, right?'

Now Manny was in a bind. She hadn't told Gulshan yet that she was waking up to a whole new meaning of fatherhood, thanks to his interactions with Erika. She wasn't ready to admit that. So she just said, 'Carry on.'

'So now let me ask you, what trade off would you need to make to live with me?' continued Gulshan.

'I'd have to leave my husband and take Erika away from her father,' said Manny, getting a bit flustered because she didn't know where the conversation was going. 'I've said that before, haven't I?'

'Sure,' said Gulshan. 'Now tell me what you would gain if you chose to live with me?'

'Hmm, well, I would have a great partner, someone I love, and I would be able to do heaps of stuff I can't do now,' said Manny.

'Like what,' said Gulshan.

'Like travel, dine out, wake up in your arms, oh come on now, stop teasing me,' said Manny.

'What about Erika,' said Gulshan. 'What would she gain?'

Manny had to answer honestly.

'I guess she'd have a father who's hands on, who spends time showing her stuff and doing things with her, who's there for her,' said Manny.

That was the closest Manny had come to confessing that she really thought that Gulshan would make a great father.

Gulshan made a mental note of Manny's comment. He was grateful his conversations with Erika had not gone unnoticed. 'Great,' he said. 'So you're clear about the gains, and the huge difference between your present life and your potential life.'

'Manny, if you choose status quo, you'll continue to wallow in this life, and as I've explained I can't continue to be the tiny part of your life that I presently am,' continued Gulshan.

'Is that really what you want?' said Gulshan. 'We have an opportunity to be together.'

Gulshan took Manny's hands in his and looked into her eyes.

'I love you Manny,' he said, his voice overcome with emotion. 'With you by my side, there's nothing more I would ever want.'

Manny's eyes were full of tears.

'You know I want to be with you,' she started to say.

Gulshan covered her mouth with his hands.

'Hush,' he said. 'Don't say all those same dialogues. They were for yesterday. Let's sit down and chalk out a plan. How do we get you out of your present situation?'

'It won't work,' she said.

'Can you fly a plane?' asked Gulshan.

'What!' Manny exclaimed. 'What are you asking? Of course not!'

'How do you know for sure when you haven't tried?' asked Gulshan. 'It's your natural instinct to say no. You've drawn a conclusion without even processing the question. We all tend to do that.'

Manny looked at Gulshan as though he was crazy. 'So now you want me to take flying lessons?' she said.

Gulshan laughed. 'No,' he said. 'I want you to give love a chance. Your problem is that you've made the whole separation and divorce issue a big deal.'

'Isn't it a big deal?' asked Manny.

'It's a big change of life,' said Gulshan. 'But it's a happy change of life, not a sad event.'

'I promise you that getting ready to leave India will be like getting ready to go for a picnic,' continued Gulshan.

Manny made a face. 'Stop it,' she said. 'Don't trivialise the matter.'

'Don't overcomplicate the matter,' said Gulshan.

They bantered some more before Manny got fed up. 'Change the topic,' she said. She went home soon after that.

*

Gulshan missed Manny like crazy but he wanted to make a conscious effort to desist from calling her. He was deeply disturbed by the way their relationship was going, or not going.

He'd been in India for over two months and while Manny expressed a lot of love for him, she wasn't in the least bit inclined to change her present situation.

Gulshan wondered whether deep down in her mind, Manny really had no feeling for her husband. Might it be that despite the absence of intimacy, she had grown attached to him? Could a person grow accustomed to a not-so-nice-situation?

Women who suffered physically or verbally abusive husbands were very receptive to counselling to get out of their situation. The greater their suffering, the deeper was their desire for change.

Manny too, had acted swiftly to get out of her situation when Harpreet had raised his hand on her in the early years of their marriage. But now, her suffering was subtle. Her in-laws tended to gang up against her whenever she expressed her opinion. Harpreet never stood up for her.

She was put down in umpteen ways. She was sidelined in favour of her brother-in-law's wife, the family's younger daughter-in-law. She was asked to do crazy things like jot down every single rupee she spent on the household. Her in-laws thought she was from an inferior caste, albeit she was from an affluent, reputed family, and they held that against her and sometimes, dropped subtle hints about the fact to guests. Even Gulshan had heard such comments firsthand but he had never retaliated because he didn't want to antagonise her in-laws while she was still living in that home. At least he had access to the place.

Perhaps Manny's subtle suffering wasn't enough for her to want change?

Pain, Gulshan knew from experience, is a great motivator. He'd had his share of pain, and somehow, scrambled out of the situation.

But then, Gulshan thought, somewhere deep inside, he had always known himself to be a fighter. Did constitution also play a role in all this? The Manny he knew was the epitome of femininity—gentle, mild, and submissive. What saddened Gulshan was the fact that Manny had been outgoing and confident in her teens. She was fearless in the early years of her marriage, when she had travelled overseas in a bid to walk out on her husband. What had happened to her after that?

Gulshan thought about all of this. Sometimes, he felt confused. Sometimes, he thought he'd go crazy. He felt the need for help.

'I don't want to rely on just my gut feeling,' he thought. 'I don't want to ever regret my decisions.'

So, he sent a message to his counsellor overseas, asking for an online appointment. She had an empty slot and so, she gave him time for later the same day.

*

Some hours later...

'How are you doing,' asked Gulshan's counsellor.

'Not so good,' said Gulshan.

She smiled. It was a video consultation but she would have done an audio conversation if Gulshan had so wanted. He had opted for face-to-face interaction.

'Do you want to tell me why,' she asked.

'I'm seeing this woman, right,' said Gulshan.

'Yes, carry on,' she said.

'She's married but her husband and she live in separate rooms. They haven't been physically intimate in years,' said Gulshan. 'She's miserable in her marriage, she loves me, I love her, I've offered her a lifetime together but she just can't seem to pluck up the courage to walk out on her husband.'

'What excuse does she give you,' asked the counsellor.

'She has an eight year old daughter,' explained Gulshan. 'She says she doesn't want to separate her daughter from her father.'

'Oh! Why do you say she is miserable in her marriage?' asked the counsellor.

'Because her in-laws have a different mindset to hers, they are repressive and put her down,' said Gulshan.

'What about her husband?' the counsellor asked. 'She may not have a physical relationship with him but do they still communicate with each other?'

'Yes, they talk to each other. But he doesn't stand up for her when her in-laws say nasty stuff to her,' said Gulshan.

'But he doesn't put her down?' the counsellor asked.

Gulshan thought a bit. 'I think he's caught up in his own world,' said Gulshan.

'I see,' said the counsellor. 'It sounds like your lady love and her husband are adjusted to their situation.'

Gulshan thought about what the counsellor was saying.

'Is that possible?' he asked, finally.

'It is,' said the counsellor. 'If your friend is the fearful type, that's probably what the issue is.'

Gulshan leaned forward to catch her words carefully.

'Explain that to me,' he said.

'Let's assume that your friend was confident in her youth, okay?' said the counsellor.

'Yes, she was,' agreed Gulshan.

'But then at some point in her life, something went wrong with her marriage, perhaps she fell out with her husband and her in-laws, and since then they look down upon her and she has internalised that perspective.'

'Do you mean to say that she has begun to believe that what they think of her is true?' asked Gulshan.

'Yes,' said the counsellor. 'When someone you look up to or respect says that you are worthless, you tend to believe it.'

'Essentially she has allowed someone's spite to undermine her self-confidence, and at some level, that has made her fearful of standing up for herself,' the counsellor added.

'Why do you use the word spite?' asked Gulshan.

'I say spite because the world is full of people trying to pull others down. Relationships have really become very toxic. That's why we see a veritable epidemic of low self confidence and the fear of speaking up.'

'And now she is fearful...' Gulshan was thinking aloud. He wanted the counsellor to complete the sentence.

'Now she is scared to stand up for herself, and take risks even when the odds are stacked in her favour,' said the counsellor. 'Is that what you practically see?'

'Yes,' said Gulshan. 'That's what I see.'

'You know Gulshan, at the workplace and in life, fearful, timid people end up missing out on amazing opportunities because they are scared to take risks and believe they are powerless to effect change,' said the counsellor.

'So you don't think her daughter has anything to do with her decision to stay in her marriage?' asked Gulshan.

'I don't think it can be the only reason,' said the counsellor. 'If she was in a really bad spot, she'd want out with her daughter in tow. Feeling bad about negativity triggers change. The worse you feel the more effort you will invest in changing your situation.'

Gulshan sighed.

There was a lull in their conversation. The counsellor maintained a respectful silence. She could see that Gulshan was thinking things through.

'Is there no hope?' asked Gulshan. 'Is there no way to help Manny shed her fear?'

'Brains can certainly be rewired with focus,' said the counsellor. 'Mindfulness, meditation, positive self talk, positive affirmations, and other methods can help people find the confidence to get out of sticky situations. The thing is you'll only practice these techniques if there is intent to refocus.'

'And here you think the intent is missing?' asked Gulshan.

'Yes, it would seem so,' said the counsellor. 'Manny isn't 100 per cent sure she wants to get out of her present situation. One part of her genuinely wants to stay for her daughter.'

'Do you think her bad marriage will set a bad example for Erika?' asked Gulshan.

Gulshan was reminded of Naomi, a young girl he had once counselled in Australia. Naomi was of Indian origin. She lived not far from Gulshan's home and sometimes ran into him when out for a walk. They would talk and she would often pour out her woes. Gulshan was amazed to find that beneath the veneer of a happy-go-lucky teenager Naomi carried a lot of emotional baggage from her childhood. Her parents had had a very bad marriage, and then a very messy divorce, the first in the family and probably in the neighbourhood, considering the unwanted attention it attracted.

'Mum used to say that people just don't get it," she once told Gulshan. 'People couldn't understand why mum had chosen to walk out on dad. They were like, "Indians don't get divorced."'

Gulshan told the counsellor about Naomi. 'As a child, she used to sleep in the same room as her parents. She saw their daily squabbles. The poor girl got into the habit of pretending to be asleep whenever she sensed that her parents were getting into an argument. They would snap at each other and gradually, the decibels would increase as they got into a shouting match.'

'Poor child,' the counsellor agreed.

'Yes,' said Gulshan. 'Invariably every argument would end with the sound of a slap.'

The counsellor shook her head in disbelief.

'The next day, Naomi would confront her mother and ask "what happened last night?" Her mother had a standard reply. "Nothing happened," she would say. "We were just playing a game".'

'Some game,' the counsellor remarked. 'You know, what you have narrated is very typical. I see a lot of such cases where the women try to cover up. In front of society they behave as if everything is alright but behind the scenes, life is a mess.'

'All of her growing years Naomi saw men being treated as though they are superior,' Gulshan said. 'In fact, she developed no concept of love between couples because she never saw her parents interact with each other with love. The family would occasionally have dinner together, her grandparents, parents and she, and that was it. Because of her parents' poor relationship she never learned how to handle her own relationships,' he said.

The counsellor nodded wisely.

'She had a boyfriend, Alvin, but broke up with him,' said Gulshan. 'Actually, that's why she reached out to me. She was looking for a sympathetic ear to vent her feelings.'

'Naomi loved Alvin immensely but she feared his anger,' Gulshan continued. 'He expected her to behave in a certain way, and if she didn't, he'd fly off the handle. He used to tell her that she was too possessive about him and that he missed his freedom when he was around her. But he himself was very possessive of her, so possessive that it made her uncomfortable.'

'That's very typical,' the counsellor said.

'Alvin was also disrespectful,' Gulshan shared. 'He'd shout at Naomi for trivial reasons. For a long time she put up with his behaviour thinking it was normal for men to shout at women. But it didn't feel right. One day about three months ago she told him that she had had enough. Before she could walk out, he verbally abused her. Naomi was a complete wreck after that. Despite being a beautiful and an extremely hardworking, intelligent girl, her confidence was shattered.'

'She went crying to her grandmother for advice,' Gulshan narrated. 'Her grandmother advised her to accept Alvin as he was if she wanted to be with him, saying that that was what women were expected to do.'

'How terrible,' the counsellor said. 'Why didn't she go to her mum?'

'She did,' said Gulshan. 'After hearing out her grandmother she went crying to her mother who said, "Don't let him dictate to you. I put up with that nonsense for far too long and missed out on life." The anger in her mother's eyes was palpable. Naomi could feel her mother's pain.'

'Then she came crying to me, asking "Why didn't he love me the way I loved him?"' said Gulshan. 'I did everything he wanted me to, to make him happy, but still he always used to be angry. Being with him was so exhausting.'

'What did you say to her?' the counsellor asked.

'You deserve better, and no one has the right to treat you the way Alvin does,' said Gulshan.

'Excellent,' said the counsellor. 'What did she reply?'

'Where will I find someone better?'

They both burst out laughing.

'That's a sharp response,' said the counsellor. 'What did you say?'

'I asked her if she had tried,' said Gulshan. 'Her reply was interesting.'

'What did she say?' asked the counsellor.

'"Yes, I did," she said. "But it didn't go anywhere. His name was Nicholas. Sadly, I couldn't relate with his family. Once I had gone over to his place. I saw his parents kissing each other, expressing affection, it felt so surreal," she said.'

'"Why," I asked.'

'"I'd never seen anything like that, it felt confusing," she said. "I would ask myself if their normal was normal or if what I had experienced with my parents was normal. Nobody shouted in their home. Everyone spoke so respectfully with one another. Then Nicholas would ask about my parents and I really didn't know what to say."'

'She's emotionally stunted,' the counsellor said.

'"Then I met Alex," she said,' Gulshan continued.

'Well, she's really been trying to find love,' said the counsellor. 'How did it go with Alex?'

'Alex's parents had had a messy divorce, and so she could relate with his situation. She felt they had common ground but she didn't love him the way she had loved Alvin,' said Gulshan.

'When she came to see me she was in a self-pitying mode. "I wish my parents had gotten divorced when I was younger.

I wish they had settled again with someone who loved and respected them. Life would have been better for both of them, especially for my mother who, for my sake, missed out on so much. I wish mum would have set an example for me by choosing love and to live her life. Why did I never get to see mother live freely and with respect and love? Why did mum choose to be unfair to me and to her own self? In the name of society and so called cultural values they set a bad example for me. I never heard dad say a good word about mum. Life sucks."'

'Goodness me, she's really in a bad spot,' said the counsellor.

'Yes, she is,' agreed Gulshan. 'I ended up telling her about Manny. So she could see that other people struggle with their past too.'

"'I can only advise you to make a fresh start," I said to her. "Don't look for love. Let it happen. Otherwise, it's just a transaction. It lacks feeling. It's like a fake flower that may look beautiful but will never have any fragrance."'

'Did it go down well?' asked the counsellor.

'Yes, at least she said she wouldn't let anyone abuse her or treat her badly again,' said Gulshan. 'She was willing to let life flow. But she was full of hope that love would happen to her someday. She felt free after a very long time.'

'Do you think Erika will become a Naomi?' asked Gulshan, finally expressing what had been uppermost in his mind for many days.

The counsellor looked thoughtful.

'She could,' she said. 'But in India, I think she will struggle with other issues too as she grows. She could be scarred by the mindset of all the members of the household but Manny will probably only wake up to that when Erika grows a little older,' explained the counsellor.

'Why's that?' asked Gulshan.

'Because Erika will want to do things and from the sound of it, she'll be denied many opportunities,' said the counsellor. 'Oh they'll cough up money to educate her and all that. It's their outlook on life that will curtail her life choices. I doubt Erika will have the freedom to say, pursue a career of her choice or marry a man she loves.'

'Hmm,' said Gulshan. 'I think you're right.'

'Suppression can lead to depression,' said the counsellor. 'All the more so among today's youth because they have so much exposure and most learn to assert themselves fairly young in life.'

Gulshan nodded. 'I see,' he said.

'Where does that leave you?' asked the counsellor.

'I'm giving her a couple of weeks more,' said Gulshan. 'If she isn't interested, I'll get out.' 'Does that mean you're planning to return?' asked the counsellor.

'Yes,' said Gulshan.

'May I make a suggestion?' asked the counsellor.

'Yes, please,' said Gulshan.

'If you're not planning to continue the relationship long distance, please make that very clear to her,' she said.

'I'm planning to break off,' said Gulshan.

'Yes, that would be the best for you,' agreed the counsellor. 'But it will upset her world.'

Gulshan looked a bit confused.

'Look,' said the counsellor. 'You say the woman loves you, I'll take you at your word. So at some level, she will be drawing comfort from your love.'

'Oh she does, I'm sure,' said Gulshan.

'Right,' said the counsellor. 'Now, if you get out of the relationship, where does that leave her?'

'In a mess,' said Gulshan. 'No doubt about that. A few months ago when we weren't talking, lovers spat and all that, she took to drinking.'

'Precisely,' said the counsellor. 'So I'd say sit her down and explain to her that you can't carry on as you are forever, even if she isn't willing to opt out. Because the minute you're gone from her life, offline and online, she'll slip into depression.'

Gulshan sighed. 'I can't think of anything sadder,' he said. 'She would be so happy living with me. I have no doubt about that.'

'Timid people are most likely to complain and most vulnerable to depression,' said the counsellor. 'It's natural, isn't it? They don't have the motivation to go after what they want and so they end up feeling depressed.'

'I see,' said Gulshan. 'I'll definitely tell her. Thank you for your advice.'

*

Manny had pinged Gulshan while he was in conversation with the counsellor. He had messaged her back saying he was on another call. As soon as he got off the call with the counsellor he called her back. 'Hi,' he said.

'Hi,' said Manny. 'What's up? Erika had wanted to talk to you.'

'I'm sorry I missed her,' said Gulshan. 'Is she around now?'

'No, she's gone out to play now,' said Manny. 'Umm, are we meeting this week?'

'Yes,' said Gulshan, sounding happy she had asked. 'Did you have anything special in mind? Need to talk about something?'

Gulshan always hoped against hope that Manny may be ready to take a step towards being together.

'No,' said Manny. 'I was just asking.'

'Is Thursday afternoon okay,' asked Manny.

'Of course,' said Gulshan. 'You'll come over?'

'Yes,' she said.

*

The next day was Wednesday.

Erika insisted on calling Gulshan in the afternoon.

'Uncle Gulshan, you're my best friend,' she said.

'I'm honoured, baby,' he said, hoping that Manny was listening.

'Is mummy around?' Gulshan asked.

'Yes, Uncle,' said the little one.

'Uncle, you and Kareena, both of you are my best friends,' said Erika.

'I'm honoured to hear so,' said Gulshan. 'You're my special friend too.'

'Uncle Gulshan, we'll be going in a plane you know,' said Erika. 'You also came in a plane? I'm so excited.'

'Plane?' said Gulshan, somewhat surprised. 'Who's going in a plane? Where are you going?'

'Daddy, mummy, and me,' said Erika. 'We're going to Goa next month.'

'Oh!' said Gulshan. 'Are you going on a holiday? Well, aren't you one lucky girl.'

'Yes Uncle, but I wish you could come too,' she said.

Gulshan laughed.

In the background, he could hear Manny asking Erika to hang up as it was time to leave for her tennis class.

'Okay Uncle, bye for now,' said Erika.

'Take care, baby' said Gulshan. 'Play some good strokes.'

*

The next afternoon Gulshan ushered Manny into his study. She strolled in and flopped down on the sofa.

'You look annoyed,' remarked Gulshan. 'What's bugging you?'

'Oh! I'm so fed up with Nimisha, you know, my sister-in-law,' she said.

'Why?' asked Gulshan. 'Did anything special happen?'

'She ordered a whole heap of stuff for the house without even asking me, all sorts of soft furnishings,' said Manny. 'The thing is, now my husband says that she's spent enough, there's no need for me to buy more. At least I could have been consulted.'

Gulshan looked at Manny with great pity.

'They treat you like s***,' he said. 'When will you realise that?'

Manny looked annoyed.

'Hey, don't remind me of how I'm treated, okay,' she said. 'You should take my side.'

'Manny, hello,' said Gulshan. 'I am on your side. I love you, remember? That's why I want you to come and live with me.'

Strangely Manny continued to look annoyed.

Gushan continued in a softer tone. 'Manny, why don't we discuss our plan,' he suggested. 'Isn't it high time we finalised something?

'I've told you before, haven't I,' said Manny. 'I can't take Erika away from her father.'

Gulshan was finding it hard to carry on, he loved Manny but he knew the conversation had to be completed.

'Right,' he said. 'So where does that leave us?'

Manny said nothing. She just played with the end of her scarf.

Gulshan started to feel annoyed. 'Manny, I think you owe it to me to listen,' he said. He hoped he wasn't sounding pompous because that wasn't his aim. He just wanted to get a message through to Manny.

Manny looked at Gulshan, surprised at his choice of words.

'Go on,' she said. 'Have your say.'

Now her choice of words offended Gulshan.

'What's with you?' asked Gulshan. 'I care for you, Manny.'

Again, she said nothing.

'Manny, I'll have to return at some point, life must go on,' said Gulshan.

'Of course,' she said. 'But you'll visit again?'

'That's the point,' said Gulshan. 'I may visit India, I don't know if and when but as for us...' and his voice trailed off.

'What about us?' Manny asked. 'We'll continue to be in touch, right?'

'I'm always just a phone call away for you, if you should ever need assistance,' said Gulshan.

Manny looked confused.

'Uh-huh,' she said.

'What I'm trying to say is that if your final decision is to stick it out, to stay with Harpreet, then I need to find the courage to move on,' said Gulshan.

'You need to find courage?' said Manny. It was a statement as well as a question.

'Yes, Manny, what did you think? That you're the only one who struggles with choices? Do you know how difficult it will be for me to let you have your way? But you must know one thing...'

Manny looked at him expectantly.

Gulshan spoke very slowly. 'When-I-get-back-I-will-not-be-around-to-chat-like-we-do-now. I-need-to-move-on.'

Manny sat very quietly, as if she was letting the full meaning of Gulshan's sentences sink in.

'You mean, we will not chat or meet?' said Manny.

Gulshan threw up his hands. 'It's your choice,' he said. 'You've done that to us. It's either a full on relationship or no relationship. Having said that, I repeat, I'm always a phone call away should you be ready for me.'

In a very low voice, he said, 'I can't take more uncertainty, Manny. I can't share you with your husband. The time has come when you must choose one of us.'

Manny's eyes opened wide at that. She looked at Gulshan, blinked and shook her head. She looked very confused.

Gulshan softened up. 'My love, I hope to God that you will not lose your sanity when we part.'

'Sanity,' she whispered. 'I'll go crazy without you Gulshan, you must know that?'

'Manny, my love, I simply can't understand why you would choose your present life over abundant joy,' said Gulshan. 'It must be my failing. If I had understood, perhaps I could have changed your mind. I always thought my love would be enough for you...'

Gulshan was extremely overcome with emotion.

'Don't ever think this is easy for me, Manny, don't ever think that,' he said.

Manny looked so lost that Gulshan just wanted to sweep her up in his arms and hug her. He ought not to, he thought. But how could he not, he thought, when she sat before him weeping. In two quick strides Gulshan stepped towards Manny and raised her up, and enveloped her in a bear hug.

'I could shake you for what you've done to me,' he said, in a voice full of emotion. 'Why did you let me love you Manny if you didn't have the guts to love me back in front of the world? Why?'

He buried his face in her neck, and started to kiss her gently first, and then as his passion grew, with a sense of urgency.

'How will we live without each other, Manny?' he said over and over again. 'How will you live without love?'

Manny wept and wept. They clung to each. Lovers. Friends. For now. But forever? Who knew? Were Manny and Gulshan destined to drift apart because of Manny's mindset?

*

Beep. Beep.

Gulshan's phone rang. He checked it out. A message from Manny.

'May we meet this afternoon?

It was Friday morning.

'Of course,' Gulshan typed back. 'Will that be the same time? 2.30pm?'

'Yes,' she replied.

Gulshan wondered what was up. Manny rarely met with him on two successive days. He had to be patient.

Bang at 2.30pm Gulshan ushered Manny into his study.

'One of these days I'll get caught,' she said.

'Are you worried about that?' he asked.

Manny changed the topic.

'Do you know yesterday my cousin dropped by and Erika said, "Uncle Gulshan is my best friend",' she said. 'My cousin was like, "Who's Uncle Gulshan?" Erika said, "Oh! You don't know Uncle Gulshan, so sad!" My cousin was so surprised. He was asking me about you.'

Gulshan smiled indulgently.

'I'm happy to meet your cousin any day,' he said.

'We'll see about that,' she said. 'What I wanted to ask you is, can you teach me finance?'

Gulshan smiled. 'I'd be happy to,' he said. 'What's up, by the way?'

'Nothing right now,' she said. 'But I think it's high time I figured out how to manage money. What if I have to someday...' her voice trailed off.

Gulshan looked thoughtful.

'What's up?' he reiterated. 'You've been doing some heavy duty thinking, haven't you?'

Manny nodded. 'I see your point about security,' she said. 'Also, Erika...'

'What about Erika?' said Gulshan. 'Is she okay?'

'Yes, she's fine. She desperately wants to meet you. Why don't you come over for dinner tomorrow?'

'I'll come,' said Gulshan. 'What excuse will you give Harpreet for calling me over?'

'I'm calling my cousin Birinder, he's one of the few people in my family who my in-laws interact with, probably the only male,' she said.

'Righto,' said Gulshan. 'What were you saying about Erika?'

'The way Erika has taken to you has got me thinking,' said Manny. 'She really likes you.'

'Hey, the feeling is mutual,' said Gulshan.

'Yes, I can see that,' said Manny with a smile. 'I must admit, I never realised that Erika misses having an elderly masculine figure in her life. I mean... she has her father but you know what I mean.'

'I do,' said Gulshan. 'I must admit, I'm glad you have realised the value I bring to Erika's life. I'd bring a lot more value to her life if you'd let me Manny.'

'Let's see what happens,' she said.

'Wow!' said Gulshan. 'That's some change from "I'm never taking Erika away from her father".'

'Well, I have been thinking,' said Manny.

'Uh-huh,' said Gulshan. 'What have you been thinking about?'

'Remember I once asked your opinion about me shifting back home?'

'Yes,' said Gulshan. 'I remember. Are you thinking of going back home? I hope with Erika?'

'No, I'm not thinking of going back home but of moving out,' said Manny. 'With Erika,' she added.

'Where do you plan to stay?' asked Gulshan.

'Some place on rent, I need to think this through,' she said.

Gulshan knew that Manny was by no means financially independent. But he also knew that she was a self-respecting woman who would die rather than take monetary support from anyone. Still he felt compelled to offer assistance.

'Sweetheart, I'll teach you whatever you need to know about managing money,' he said. 'But have you worked out where the money to live on will come from?'

'I have a few ideas,' said Manny.

Gulshan sighed.

'Manny, I'd be happy to take a place on rent and furnish it for you,' he said. 'It's the least I can do to help you settle down.'

Gulshan hoped that Manny wouldn't misconstrue his offer. Hopefully she was in a better space now.

Manny looked at Gulshan thoughtfully.

'Manny you may not be ready to accept me in front of the world but perhaps you're ready to accept me as a well-wisher?' said Gulshan.

'I'll consider your suggestion,' she said.

Gulshan thought that that was a big comedown for Manny. He decided to leave it at that. 'I'll get you a good book on managing finances,' he said.

'Oh no,' said Manny. 'I don't want to read a book. You just point me in the right direction.'

'Okay, I'll give you whatever tips I can,' said Gulshan. 'Let me start right away.'

They spent the next hour in deep discussion. Gulshan explained to Manny the need for financial planning to cover savings, investments, medical expenses, emergencies, and life protection.

Manny made a few notes. She was very serious about learning, Gulshan was happy to note.

*

Manny ushered Gulshan into the living room. Birinder was already sitting there with Harpreet.

Gulshan shook hands with Birinder and Harpreet.

Birinder was observing Gulshan very keenly. Gulshan thought he knew why. Birinder's curiosity in him was triggered by Erika's comment about Uncle Gulshan.

Just then Gulshan heard a shriek, an exclamation of happiness. It was Erika. She had come running down the stairs to meet Uncle Gulshan, her best friend.

She entered the living room on the trot and made a beeline for Gulshan. He stood up to greet her. She clearly wanted a hug and that was what she got. A bear hug from Uncle Gulshan.

Birinder smiled to see their bonding. Harpreet looked faintly displeased. He looked at Manny as if to say, 'Why is she behaving that way?'

Manny shrugged her shoulders. What could she do? It didn't seem fair to ask Erika to behave like a mannequin. She was just being a regular child.

'Uncle Gulshan, you're my best friend,' Erika said beaming away to glory.

Harpreet looked decidedly embarrassed. Manny looked at Birinder to see the effect of Erika's words on him. He looked amused.

'Erika, don't you have homework to do?' Harpreet asked.

'No daddy, I've done my homework,' she said. 'I want to sit with Uncle Gulshan now.'

Erika's voice was firm.

Harpreet's disapproval was written large on his face. Children should be seen and not heard, that was his line of thinking.

Just then Nimisha entered the room. She quickly took in the scene. Erika was sitting with Gulshan on a single seater. Gulshan had his arm around her protectively. Erika was avidly telling Gulshan about her latest tennis class.

Gulshan politely smiled at Nimisha and folded his hands to greet her, without getting up as he didn't want to interrupt Erika.

Nimisha seemed miffed about that. She looked at Manny disapprovingly, as if to say, 'Can't you control your daughter?'

Manny looked studiously away. She was feeling slightly rebellious. Birinder motioned to her to sit next to him. Manny went over and sat beside him.

'It's great to see her opening up like that,' said Birinder. 'I don't recollect her ever being so chatty and happy before.'

Manny nodded. 'I agree,' she said.

'Erika, don't you have homework to do?' asked Nimisha. Gulshan was deep in conversation with Erika but like everyone else in the room he heard Nimisha. He was amused as well as disgusted by Harpreet and Nimisha's attitude.

Feeling very protective about Erika he took over the conversation. He laughed and politely said to Nimisha, 'Her father asked exactly the same thing a few minutes ago. She's done her homework, and I'm enjoying our chat.'

Well! Gulshan was their guest and out of politeness, they needed to go along with whatever his preference was.

Erika looked a bit confused. Clearly, she wasn't as comfortable replying her aunt as she had been replying her father.

To put her at ease, Gulshan whispered in her ear: 'You're not getting bored with our chat, are you baby?'

'Uncle Gulshan!' exclaimed Erika. 'No way, I love talking to you.'

'Me too, baby,' said Gulshan.

Hearing that, Erika relaxed. She beamed at Gulshan. She looked as if she wanted another hug. She seemed overwhelmed with love for Gulshan. She lovingly rested her head against him. Gulshan stroked her head.

Nimisha looked increasingly angry at their display of affection.

Turning to Harpreet Gulshan said, 'You're a very lucky man, you have a lovely daughter. I'm enjoying her company today but you get to be with her every day.'

Harpreet looked as though he didn't know what to say.

Birinder looked amused. It wasn't as if he knew about Manny's situation with her husband. No one in her family did. But yes, he knew that Manny's in-laws were formal in their outlook and she had to mind her P's and Q's around them. He could see that Erika was relating with Gulshan so well and he doubted that Harpreet had ever had a similar affectionate moment with his daughter.

'Shall we move to the table?' said Nimisha. She was visibly annoyed about the way the evening was panning out.

'Sure,' said Gulshan. He stood up and held Erika hand in his. 'After you,' he said politely to Nimisha.

Nimisha led the way to the dining table. It was set for five people.

Nimisha, Harpreet, Manny, Gulshan, Birinder.

Nimisha looked pointedly at Manny and then at Erika. 'Shouldn't someone be in bed by now?' she said.

Gulshan looked at Harpreet and said, 'This is a six-seater table, if you would allow me the privilege of sitting near your daughter, I would be most obliged.'

Harpreet was taken aback. He didn't want to be rude to Gulshan so he merely nodded, and then looked at Manny and asked her to set the table for one more person. Manny quickly gave the servant instructions to bring crockery and cutlery for one more person.

Gulshan could feel Erika shiver probably out of fear of her aunt. He squeezed her hand. She looked up at him with her eyes wide open. When he was sure that no one was looking at him, he winked at Erika.

Birinder saw the exchange. He was tickled. When Nimisha got busy saying something to Harpreet, Birinder whispered to Manny, who was sitting next to him, 'Erika should spend more time with Gulshan, he's so good with her.'

Manny smiled.

Manny had decided on a continental menu with a number of dishes, including penne pasta and vegetables done separately.

'I don't like veggies,' said Erika, making a face. 'Can't I have pasta with tomato ketchup?'

Manny reached out to pass her the ketchup but Gulshan stopped her. 'Give me a chance to talk to her about veggies,' he said.

Turning to Erika, Gulshan asked, 'Baby, can you count the colours on this plate?' He held the plate of veggies in his hand.

'Hmm,' said Erika. 'So there's red...' she said.

'Tell me the name of the veggie too,' said Gulshan.

'But I don't know the names of the veggies,' Erika wailed.

'Well that's too bad,' said Gulshan. 'Let's see, you say the colour and I'll tell you the name of the veggie. Like a game.'

Erika started to look excited about the exercise.

'So there's red...' she said, and looked expectantly at Gulshan.

'Red capsicum,' said Gulshan.

'Yellow...' she said.

'Yellow capsicum,' said Gulshan.

'Green...' she said.

'Broccoli,' said Gulshan. 'Also, beans.'

'Orange...' she said.

'Come on, that's an easy one, you tell me which veggie that is,' said Gulshan.

'Carrots,' said Erika, and she was so excited by now that her voice rose by several decibels.

At the other end of the table Nimisha stood up, 'Manny this isn't right, I've had enough, the least you can do is to control your daughter.'

Gulshan was shocked to hear Nimisha's outburst. He put a hand up to prevent Manny from saying anything.

Looking squarely at Nimisha, he said, 'In my family, we sit down to eat together and enjoy each other's company. Meals are an opportunity to bond. I'm sorry if you think otherwise.'

Nimisha looked dumbstruck. She shrugged her shoulders as if to close the conversation. She turned around and walked out of the room.

Gulshan turned to Erika, 'What I was going to say baby, is that it would be very nice if you would try to eat these very colourful veggies. Did you know that each colour stands for a certain vitamin and mineral, stuff that is good for your growth?'

'No,' said Erika, again with her eyes open wide. She looked at the plate of veggies with a newfound respect. 'May I have some veggies please,' she said.

'Of course you may,' said Gulshan. He served Erika some veggies.

Manny looked thrilled.

Birinder looked amused.

Harpreet looked as if he didn't know whether he approved or not.

The rest of the dinner passed off peacefully. There was no sign of Nimisha.

The elders had all enjoyed a glass of wine with the pasta. Erika had eyed the bottle and the wine glasses. Gulshan made a note of all that. Just before they got up, he whispered to her, 'I promise to let you try some when you're a little older. Now you go to bed and we'll chat more soon. Okay?'

'Okay Uncle Gulshan,' said Erika.

Gulshan gave her a hug and looked at Manny, who took the

cue and led Erika away. She hopped along happily. It was the first time Erika had ever sat down for an evening meal with guests.

Birinder had overheard Gulshan. He laughed out loud en route to the living room, where the three men were headed. 'You're great!' he said. 'I really liked how you interacted with Erika.'

'She's playful but she doesn't get too many opportunities at home to express that side of her,' muttered Gulshan.

'Hmm,' said Birinder.

Harpreet pretended not to have heard what the two had just said. The men served themselves a drink at the bar and sat down to chat.

Manny walked in some fifteen minutes later.

Gulshan smiled at her. 'You tucked your baby in?' he asked.

'Yes,' said Manny.

'It's so important to make children feel wanted,' said Gulshan.

Harpreet started to look annoyed. Birinder's face took on the same amused look it had during the earlier part of the evening.

Beep. Beep.

Everyone looked to see whose handset was ringing. It was Harpreet's. He looked at the display and frowned. 'I'm sorry gentlemen, but I need to take this call,' he said.

'Sure,' said Gulshan.

Birinder nodded.

Harpreet took the call and walked out of the room.

Manny helped herself to a glass of wine and sat next to them, sipping.

Birinder looked at Gulshan curiously and asked, 'How did you get to be so close to Erika?'

Gulshan smiled. 'I love children,' he said.

'Come on,' said Birinder. 'Surely you aren't so close to every child you know?'

'Actually, I don't know too many children,' said Gulshan. 'But I will tell you why I got close to Erika.'

Manny looked faintly worried.

'Erika is a wonderful girl with incredible aptitude but like any child, she needs the right environment to blossom,' explained Gulshan.

Birinder nodded.

'That necessitates engaging with her family, you agree?' asked Gulshan.

'Of course,' said Birinder.

'Erika doesn't interact too much with her family, as you might have gathered,' said Gulshan. 'So I like to indulge her whenever I have a chance.'

'I see,' said Birinder. Turning to Manny he said, 'Bringing up munchkins is hard work!'

Manny just nodded.

Birinder looked as if he wanted to ask something but Harpreet entered the room just then.

'Change the topic,' Manny hissed.

'Sure,' whispered Birinder.

Birinder asked Harpreet about his work.

*

Later that night after Gulshan had got back home Manny called him. 'That was some evening,' he said.

'Yes,' Manny agreed.

'Harpreet didn't stick up for you or for Erika in front of Nimisha,' said Gulshan. 'I thought that was very inconsiderate.'

Manny didn't say anything.

'Manny?' said Gulshan. 'Don't you agree? I mean, saying something against your mother-in law is one thing, although he should speak up in front of her too, but Nimisha? Why's he scared of his sister? Why does he show himself to be weak?'

'I agree,' said Manny. 'But what's the point in saying so?'

'The point is not to say anything, Manny, the point is to do something about your situation,' said Gulshan. 'But that will only happen when you realise you need to do something.'

'What was the need to drop hints about my situation in front of Birinder?' asked Manny.

Gulshan got the feeling that Manny was purposely changing the topic.

'I didn't let on any secrets, Manny' said Gulshan. 'Did I say that your in-laws treat you like dirt?'

'No,' said Manny.

'Did you hear me tell Birinder that you've been cut out of the family business?' asked Gulshan.

'No,' said Manny.

'Did I say anything about your loveless marriage or about you and Harpreet occupying separate bedrooms?'

'No,' said Manny.

'Did you hear me say that you've got no assets in your name worth mentioning, or that you're financially fully dependent on Harpreet and get monthly dole-outs from him?' Gulshan continued.

Manny didn't say anything.

'Well?' asked Gulshan. 'Did I say anything on those lines?'

'No,' said Manny.

'Mostly we were talking about Erika; now don't tell me that you have a problem with that too?' asked Gulshan.

'No,' said Manny.

'Great,' Gulshan said. 'Because it's time you started to think about Erika. Your in-laws will make mince of her if you do nothing. I hope you noticed the lack of interest in making her happy.'

'I did,' said Manny.

'Today, it's a child battling needless reprimands, tomorrow it'll be a teenager struggling to make sense of human relationships,' said Gulshan.

'I wish you wouldn't say that,' said Manny.

'Why?' asked Gulshan. 'Do you really think that Erika will be unaffected by your relationship with Harpreet and by living in a toxic environment?'

'Who knows,' said Manny.

'Come on, Manny,' said Gulshan. 'Remember what you were saying the other day? About spending time in a toxic environment rubbing off on you, making you angry? And sadly, you sometimes vent your frustration on Erika?'

'Yes but...' said Manny.

'Look I'm sure Erika will sooner or later start to feel discomforted by your situation,' said Gulshan. 'She's a sensitive child, she's sure to pick up your vibes soon.'

'Oh well,' said Manny. 'Let's see, I'm thinking a lot these days.'

'I hope you're thinking of good things,' said Gulshan. 'Your life could turn 180 degrees, you know?'

'Yes,' said Manny. 'It all depends on what I choose.'

'True,' said Gulshan. 'I, you, everyone is a product of choices we made in the past. I guess that's inspiration to choose well today.'

Sitting alone in her room Manny smiled but all she said was 'Good night.'

'Good night sweetheart,' replied Gulshan.

*

The next day Gulshan sat in his study sipping coffee, reflecting over recent events.

Manny's thoughts had oscillated between optimism and pessimism. Of late she had been a lot more optimistic. That had given him hope for a positive resolution. He wondered if she was busy.

Beep. Beep.

Gulshan's phone rang. He looked at the display. It was Manny.

Gulshan smiled. That was how connected they were.

'Hi,' he said, feeling upbeat.

'Hi,' she said, sounding bothered.

'What's up?' Gulshan asked.

'I just received a call from Erika's school,' said Manny. 'Schools are reopening. There's so much to do. I need to take her shopping for a new uniform and other stuff.'

'I'm happy to hear that,' said Gulshan. 'Erika will be ecstatic to meet her friends. Home schooling isn't a patch on the real thing.'

'Oh but I'll miss having her around,' said Manny. 'I've gotten so used to her being home and guiding her study.'

'Manny,' said Gulshan. 'Get real. She needs to go to school. You'll still be with her in the afternoon and evening.'

There was a lull in their conversation.

'I don't like being alone,' said Manny.

Gulshan thought that Manny had really taken the situation to heart. 'Manny,' he said gently. 'What'll you do when Erika grows up?'

'Don't hassle me,' she said.

Gulshan laughed. 'Sweetheart, I didn't mean to hassle you,' he said. 'I was just nudging you to think. That's what I've been doing these last few weeks, isn't it.'

'Yes,' agreed Manny. 'And I have been thinking heaps.'

'Yes, I know you have,' said Gulshan. 'You said so yesterday as well. Thinking becomes easier when you have a clear picture of where you stand.'

'Oh I know where I stand,' said Manny.

'I'm sure you do,' said Gulshan. 'So?'

'So what,' Manny asked, sounding annoyed.

'Do we have a decision?' Gulshan asked.

For about thirty seconds there was quiet. Gulshan was about to prod Manny when she snapped, 'I've told you a hundred times that I cannot walk out. Stop bringing up the subject again and again. It stresses me.'

'Where did that come from?' wondered Gulshan. He was taken aback by her outburst and the anger that was palpable in her voice but he kept quiet. Internally he thought, 'It's time for me to return. She says I add to her stress? What about my feelings?'

'You know what?' said Manny, seemingly oblivious to the turmoil in Gulshan's head.

'What?' said Gulshan, wondering what was coming next.

'You should go back,' said Manny.

'Right,' thought Gulshan. 'I agree. It is time for me go back. At least I will not be around to add to her stress. That's the last thing on my mind. If she wants me to go, I'll go even though I'll suffer from being away from her. I'll miss us.'

When Gulshan didn't reply, Manny simply said, 'Good night.'

'Good night,' said Gulshan.

*

The very next day Gulshan booked a ticket back home. He had just a week more in the city. He texted Manny to tell her.

"Took your advice. Booked my ticket. Departing seven days from today."

Manny called him about 30 seconds after he hit 'Send'.

'You're going?' she exclaimed. 'Why? Why are you leaving so soon?'

'Last night you suggested that I return,' said Gulshan.

'But... but...,' Manny was at a loss for words then it all came tumbling out. 'What'll I do without you?' she said.

157

'Excuse me?' said Gulshan.

'What'll I do without you?' repeated Manny.

'Manny, my love, you know why I'm going back,' said Gulshan. 'It hasn't been easy being in my position.'

'When will you visit again?' asked Manny.

'The day you send me a message saying you're ready for me, for us, I'll hop onto the next available flight,' said Gulshan.

'Whaaat?' said Manny.

'Manny, we all need closure,' said Gulshan. 'Harpreet, Erika, you, me. You need to decide what's good for everyone. Perhaps some time and space will help you decide if you want to be with me.'

'No one has ever loved me as much as you have,' said Manny.

'Now that's something I agree with,' said Gulshan, trying his best to be light.

'And you not being around will be such a loss for Erika,' continued Manny. 'She'll miss her conversations with Uncle Gulshan.'

Gulshan sighed. He worried about Manny but he knew that true loves needs patience.

'She'll have to cope as best as she can,' he thought. 'It's her choice after all. What can I do beyond wishing her well?'

With a heavy heart, Gulshan steeled himself for the parting that seemed inevitable for now. Walking away from you is the most difficult thing I've ever done, Manny, my love.

Epilogue

What makes *Manny, My Love* a special story is the fact that Manny and Gulshan are real people.

Manny has yet to make up her mind about her future. She's caught up with what's right and wrong in the eyes of society. She worries about social ostracisation should she walk out of her marriage to live with Gulshan. She believes her daughter will be more secure with her biological father. Such thoughts founded in fear are holding her back from getting together with Gulshan despite loving him deeply.

Gulshan, on the other hand, is clear. He wants nothing more than to spend the rest of his life with Manny and Erika. That's why he went out of his way to show Manny what a good life she, Erika, and he could have.

It's very frustrating to love someone who isn't willing to openly accept you as a lover. It's hurtful to see your love prefer a life of suppression and insults over freedom and happiness. While Gulshan has pledged to always be there for Manny, should she need support to get out of her stifling present circumstances, he's decided to step aside from her to protect his own heart.

It takes two hearts to keep a relationship going. Gulshan has done his bit. Now it's upto Manny and Manny alone to express the desire to solemnise their love.

Having read *Manny, My Love*, perhaps you have developed an opinion on whether Manny should walk out of her dead marriage to enjoy a lifetime with Gulshan? Or, perhaps you can opine on how long Gulshan should wait for Manny to make up her mind? Do you think Erika's mental and emotional growth will be stifled if Manny stays in a loveless marriage?

Share your views with Gulshan and Manny @ www.MannyMyLove.com Get regular updates on their story as it unfolds.

Printed in Great Britain
by Amazon

74238436R00099